MAX, THE SEQUEL

MAX, THE SERIES #2

BEY DECKARD

Bey
Deckard
Books

CONTENTS

To Dr. M.
Without you, I wouldn't have been inspired to write these deranged books.

BEHOLD: CONTENT WARNINGS

If you've read the first book (and if you haven't . . . you really, really should), you can guess what sort of things to expect, but I'll put some content warnings here anyway:

Lies, cheating, substance abuse, more lies, dubious consent, abuse (including nondetailed mentions of child abuse), all sorts of mindfuckery, lies (did I already mention lies?), angst, amputation, crime . . . and a tiny pink bikini (is this really a content warning . . . or a promise?).
Oh, and lies.

AUTHOR'S NOTE

Ask, and you shall receive.
Well . . . Eventually. ;)

Damn, this was fun to write.

SOUNDTRACK

http://geni.us/Max2OST

ONE
THE SETUP

Crane blinked slowly as he lifted his head. He was groggy and still half dreaming, and for a few confusing seconds, he thought he was on a school bus. But he wasn't on a bus . . . he was sitting on a chair in a small stuffy room. Sunshine poked through rips in the paper covering the window, and narrow shafts of light streaked the gloom—his breath made the motes of dust whirl and dance in and out of the bright beams. To the left were metal shelves, bare except for a few cracked terracotta pots; to the right, a long workbench was covered in a jumble of metal objects. Crane squinted, his head pounding, and saw a hammer, pliers . . . a few screwdrivers.

A . . . toolshed?

Why was he in a toolshed? And why did it feel like his brain wanted to leak out of his ears? What the hell had happened?

He went to rub his head and made another discovery: he was *tied* to the chair with a thick leather belt around his midsection, pinning his arms to his sides.

"What the fuck?" he whispered, his mouth pasty and foul. "Hello?"

"Doc?"

"Max, what the fuck is going on?" Crane said, trying to look over his shoulder. He could make out a few curls of Max's dark hair—they were seated back-to-back on metal chairs, the young man no doubt tied like he was. "Max?"

"Yeah, I'm here."

"Are you all right?" Crane asked, straining against the belt, trying to free himself. He looked over his shoulder again when Max hadn't said anything. "You okay?"

"I'm all right," came the quiet reply.

Relieved, Crane glanced over at the tools, wondering for a moment if he could reach something with his foot, but who was he kidding? There was no way he'd get his leg up that high. Closing his eyes, Crane licked his lips, trying not to panic. Were they about to be tortured? Executed?

The air in the shed was hot and heavy with humidity. It was like sitting in a sauna; every stifling breath felt saturated with moisture. Panting, Crane tried to shift the leather belt around his middle, but he couldn't get it to budge even the tiniest bit. He could grab it with his hands, but that didn't give him the leverage to move it.

"Goddammit . . ." Changing tack, he planted his feet to either side of the chair legs, leaned forward as far as he could, grabbed the seat, and tried to stand. However, the chair wouldn't budge. He grunted as he attempted a second time, but it felt like the chair was bolted to the floor. It was a permanent fixture, a torture chair in a creepy little toolshed. He let out two rapid, shallow breaths as sweat poured down his forehead, dripping from the end of his nose, and cleared his throat, preparing to shout.

As if reading his mind, Max spoke up. "I don't think you should yell. Who knows who'll come running?"

"Right . . . right." Crane bowed his head, thinking, but all that kept coming to mind was the torture scene in *Reservoir Dogs* set to "Stuck in the Middle with You."

No clowns to the left, no jokers to the right, but a sociopath at my back . . . Crane gave a little giggle, tears springing to his eyes, and finally, the panic broke through.

First, he groaned and frantically began rocking and shaking, scratching at the leather belt, then he kicked out his legs and twisted his arms as far as they would go, his heart going like a John Bonham solo until his shirt was completely soaked through with sweat. When he realized there was absolutely nothing he could do to escape his predicament, he sagged in the chair, his eyes closed.

After he'd caught his breath, he felt oddly calm.

"All right . . ." he said with a sigh. "Now what?"

TWO
THE VERY BEGINNING
FOUR WEEKS EARLIER

TUESDAY, NOVEMBER 7TH

Crane deposited the cloth grocery bag on the narrow kitchen island and put the milk in the fridge along with the beer. After a thought, he added the bread. He wondered if it would keep better in there than on the counter. At the very least, the ants wouldn't get to it.

A bottle of white wine was chilling in the fridge door, and Crane smiled. It was obviously a peace offering . . . Max never felt *bad* about anything, but he was getting better at apologizing.

"Max?" he called out, kicking off his flip-flops. He put his straw fedora next to Max's and walked towards the balcony. He was probably outside sunbathing. "Hello?"

"In here," Max called from the bedroom.

Frowning, Crane pushed the door open and stopped in his tracks, his magnanimity extinguished completely by the scene he was greeted with.

On the bed was a young woman, a teenager really,

sprawled out naked on her back, her legs splayed wide. Clad only in a bright-purple T-shirt, Max had one hand stuffed inside the girl's vagina, the other wrapped around his erection. The girl looked passed out . . . or dead.

"Hi, baby," Max said brightly. "Did you pick up some beer . . . and . . . uh, some cleaning products?"

"What the *hell* are you doing?" Crane said in a low voice.

Max blinked at him, the smile freezing on his face. He glanced over at the girl. "Uh—" He pulled his hand halfway out of her and raised his brows. "I'm cooking a chicken," he said, turning his gaze back on Crane. "What does it *look* like I'm doing."

The girl let out a low giggle and turned her head, proving herself alive, if not wholly conscious. Crane watched her perky little breasts move with her breathing.

"Did you drug her?" Crane asked in a tight voice.

"No," Max replied. He drew his hand completely out, leaving the girl's anatomy a gaping pink cavern for a brief instant before she groaned and turned on her side. Max crossed his heart, his wet finger darkening the purple of his shirt. "Promise."

"Then what's wrong with her?" The room smelled of sex —he could taste the young woman's scent in the back of his throat. *Pussy, Doc. Cunt.* Crane swallowed, wiping his lips with the back of his wrist.

"Oh, hey, I think she fell asleep," Max answered.

"Before or after you started . . . uh, doing . . . *that?*"

"Bit of both?" Max grinned, his eyes narrowing. "Hey, you want to throw a quick fuck into her before she goes? It's okay; she won't mind. I know I've got a bit of a head start, but—"

"No." Crane was appalled. He took a small step back and straightened his spine. "What I want is her *out* of here."

"Awww, *Doc*," Max said, his shoulders slumping. "But . . . I thought maybe we could share her, you know?"

"No."

"You're such a stick in the mud." Max crossed his arms and jutted out his bottom lip like a cranky toddler.

"We had an agreement: *you don't bring anyone home*," Crane said, jabbing a finger in the direction of the young woman.

She was rather pretty, even in her dishevelled state—olive-skinned with thick, wavy black hair, high cheekbones, and full lips—almost model pretty, but good god, she seemed young.

"What is she, a hooker?" He realized just as he said it that he had no idea whether prostitution was legal in Mexico, and La Quinta Avenida, the main tourist drag a block over, was crawling with cops. "Please tell me she's not a hooker."

"Doc, she's not a *hooker*. Gosh, what do you take me for? Why would I bother with a—"

"Max!" Crane said, his tone sharp with impatience. "I don't care. Just get her out."

"*Fine.*" Max threw himself back hard on the bed and turned his head away, his transformation into a sulky child complete. "But you can carry her out yourself."

"What do you mean, *carry*? I thought you said she was going. Wake her up!"

"I said before she *goes* and"—Max sat up and pinched one of the girl's nipples hard with no response—"and it looks like she's *gone*." He clucked his tongue, shaking his head.

"Wake her up."

"Doc, I *can't*. She's totally drugged out. I'd be amazed if she woke up before, like . . . six."

"I thought you didn't drug her."

"I said *I* didn't drug her. She did all this to herself."

"Jesus fucking Christ, Max," Crane said softly. This time, he kept the anger out of his voice, opting for weary disappointment. For some reason, that always worked better with Max. "Just . . . get her dressed and get her the hell out of here."

Max turned to face him, his dark eyes flinty, and Crane stared back, holding his ground. Finally, Max sighed and leaned over the side of the bed to rifle through the discarded clothing on the floor, looking for items belonging to the young woman. When he began dressing her, he did it with little care, jerking her around like a lifeless doll with her head flopping forward and back as he manhandled her bra into place. With a grin, he looked over at Crane and squeezed the sleeping woman's breasts through the lacy black material. "Nice, huh?" He bit his bottom lip mischievously. "Are you *sure* you don't wanna—"

"*Max.*"

Muttering to himself, Max began working the woman's panties up her legs.

Crane stood there watching for another minute, then turned and walked to the kitchen, snagging a glass, the corkscrew, and the bottle of wine from the fridge, and headed out to the balcony. He set the glass on the small plastic table and got to work opening the bottle. Below, the beach was teeming with tourists. A large man in a fedora at least two sizes too small stopped and glanced up at Crane, holding his gaze for a few seconds before disappearing into the throng of beachgoers, and Crane sighed, missing their previous location. That beach had been *far* less crowded—but he did have to admit this condo was a step up from the last place. They were on the top floor of the building and the only ones with a large partially covered balcony. Unless they were standing right at the railing like he was, the balcony was private, and that suited Crane just fine—he was on the lam, after all, which was why it pissed him off to no end that Max continuously drew attention to them. He clenched his jaw and shook his head.

The cork came out easily with a soft *pop*, and Crane sighed and sat down, sipping at the cold Chilean Chardonnay.

Yeah. Right. That's *why you're angry. Keep lying to yourself.* Crane let out a slow breath and concentrated on the single white cloud in the otherwise pristine blue sky as the tired old ceiling fan above creaked and groaned through its revolutions, lending little in the way of a breeze.

He was on his second glass when he heard the condo door open and Max leave only to return a few minutes later, speaking in Spanish with someone. Frowning, he listened hard and caught the word *taxi*. Max must have gone down to the stand at the corner to get a cabbie to help him take the young woman downstairs. Besides the words *taxi* and *chica*, Crane couldn't understand what they were saying. Max made learning a new language look so easy—Crane could only get around Playa del Carmen because of the sizeable English-speaking tourist trade, but Max was nearly fluent, which meant Crane had to rely on him for almost everything, which was . . . well, irksome, if not downright frightening.

The taxi driver started sounding agitated, and Max's voice took on that soft, cajoling note it did when he was trying to convince someone to do something for him. Finally, the man agreed, and after a long silence, Crane heard a heavy tread and the door to the condo close.

He shut his eyes and took another deep breath.

"Hey," came the quiet voice from the patio door. "Doc?"

Crane opened his eyes but didn't look at Max. Instead, he leaned forward to pour himself some more Chardonnay. "How old was she?"

"Old enough. I promise."

Snorting, Crane shook his head. "You also promised not to bring anyone home."

"Yeah, I know. I just thought—"

"*No.* I don't want to come home to a scene like that again. Do I make myself clear?" He turned to Max.

Max had thrown on a pair of yellow board shorts and ditched the purple T-shirt—Crane stared at the Ouroboros on Max's chest. Meaning infinity or wholeness, it also represented cyclicality—of something constantly recreating itself. A perfect symbol for his diabolically capricious companion. He looked up and met Max's eyes, holding his gaze, unblinking.

Eventually, Max bowed his head. "Yes, Doc. I'm sorry."

"No, you aren't . . ." Crane let out a humourless chuckle. "But I know something that might help you remember for next time." He let a slow smile crease his cheeks.

Max's head jerked up, his eyes wide. "Oh no."

"Oh, *yes.* Go and get them."

It looked like Max would defy him for a moment, but then he turned on his heel and went back into the condo.

Crane sighed, his shoulders sagging, and sat back in his chair, fortifying himself with more wine. He knew it was a dangerous game he was playing. Max was only docile because it suited him—the day would come when Crane went too far, and he would pay the price. It was something that kept him up at night when he'd had too much to drink . . . or too little— the thought that one day Max would tire of him, and then what? Would Max simply abandon him? Send him back to jail? Or . . . worse? They'd never spoken of Mr. Bertrand after the night of his rescue, but Crane often wondered: had Max killed him with his own hands, or had he hired someone else to do it?

Does it really matter, Doc?

"Here," Max said, stepping out onto the balcony.

He held out a pair of black leather bondage cuffs and a matching collar, a small padlock, a chain, and a short stainless-steel hook with a large ball on one end and a fixed ring on the other.

Crane hadn't even known something like the last item existed before Max, nor that he would get so much enjoyment from using it on him. The blood was already coursing to his cock in anticipation. Punishing Max was the only way he ever felt remotely in control of his life . . . a heady, delusional fiction.

Though his pulse was racing, Crane calmly took the hook and restraints from Max and set them on the table next to his wine. He stood, adjusting himself as he got to his feet, and stared down at Max. His irises were so dark in the shade of the balcony that they were almost black—frustratingly unreadable.

Curling his lip, Crane bent and grabbed Max's shorts, yanking them down roughly to his ankles. He could still smell the woman on Max, which threw more fuel on his anger.

Standing, he leaned closer, his lips brushing the rim of Max's ear.

"When you bring *anyone* home, it puts us in danger," he said quietly through clenched teeth, one hand around the back of Max's neck.

"I know, Doc."

Crane pulled Max back by the hair and frowned down at him. He looked like he'd shaved that morning, but the dark stubble was already visible on his tanned cheeks. Perspiration began beading on Max's upper lip. Was he sweating in anticipation or dread? Would Crane ever really know?

He picked up the hook from the table and held the ball in front of Max's face. It was about two and a half inches wide. "Open"

Max took a shaky breath, his nostrils quivering, and opened his mouth as wide as he could. Crane put the ball into it, rubbing it on Max's tongue. When he was satisfied it was wet all over, he grabbed Max's shoulder to turn him around. "All right. On your knees." Crane's cock was a hot bar pulsing against his skin, trapped between the waistband of his shorts and his belly.

"I won't do it again," Max said quickly, his expression tense as if genuinely apprehensive. "I really am sorry. Honest."

Bullshit.

Max's cock hung limp, still shrouded in its wrinkled foreskin, but that meant nothing for someone who seemed to have preternatural control over his body's reactions. For all Crane knew, Max was as turned on as he was.

"Too little, too late," Crane said. "Kneel."

A deep wrinkle appeared between Max's dark brows as

he faltered, but he finally turned and sank to his knees on the concrete, leaning forward to rest his forehead on the ground. The angel on Max's back held a longsword between its hands, the pommel in the shape of a snake's head, and the blade's tip reaching the centre of his sacrum as if pointing to the pink pucker that clenched as Max shifted. He put his hands behind him, his fists white-knuckled.

Crane went down on one knee and spat on Max's hole before he pushed the ball hard against it, forcing it open.

Max let out a pained gasp.

Crane grinned as the steel ball got sucked into Max's ass.

Whimpering, Max shuddered and panted a few times, his thighs trembling. "God, that hurts."

Crane's grin got wider. "Good."

He gave his own cock a stroke through his shorts before giving Max's ass a smack that was probably heard all the way down on the beach. With a yelp, Max jerked forward, his ass cheeks squeezing together, and the tail of the hook wiggled back and forth as the ball slid a little deeper.

Bellissimo, as Max would say.

Grinning, Crane collared Max, cuffed his hands behind his back, and clipped one end of the chain to the back of the collar. He then slid the lock through the last loop of the chain and the D rings in the cuffs and tugged up on the anal hook to padlock the chain and cuffs to the ring at the top of it. The chain was barely long enough to reach, and Max groaned and huffed as it pulled the metal ball further into his body.

Now Max couldn't move without forcing the hook to go deeper, and the only way he could move at all was by crawling forward on his knees in tiny increments as he lifted his torso off the ground.

"Comfortable?" asked Crane, reclaiming his seat. Then, pocketing the key, he shoved at Max's ass with his foot. "Hm?"

"No. Not in the least," came the terse reply. Max turned his head, his cheek resting on the bare concrete. "How long?"

"I don't know. I haven't decided." Crane sipped his wine as he grasped his cock through the thick material of his shorts. "Did you take the sheets off the bed and put them in the hamper?"

Max groaned. "No, I didn't think of it."

"Did you mean for me to sleep in the filth you left behind?" Crane squinted at Max, tilting his head. Dirty sheets weren't really the issue, of course. For some reason, he got insanely jealous whenever Max even *flirted* with someone, and he was always amazed by how angry and *horny* it made him.

You've got serious problems, Doc.

Very serious problems, he thought. For one, his conscience now sounded like Max all the time. Soon, he'd be forced to take a good long look at himself and what he'd become, but he'd be happy to put that off for as long as he could.

He ran his fingers up along the bottom of his shaft, giving himself a shiver of pleasure, and gave Max another nudge with his toes. "So, did you fuck her or just use her as a hand puppet?"

A grin flashed across Max's face at his language, but he quickly schooled his features. "Yeah, I fucked her. I know . . . I know, I just—"

"Wait, did you *wear a condom?*" The thought had only just occurred to Crane, and he stopped playing with himself, his jaw clenched tight.

This time Max winced. "Um. Nope. I'm sorry. But, like I said, she's not a hooker, Doc. I don't think—"

Crane stood, furious. "Jesus Christ." His erection shrank with every beat of his heart. "How could you be so *stupid*?" He shook his head, disgusted by Max's lack of judgment. "What if you caught something . . ."

"She's really not that kind of girl, Doc," Max protested. "And you've got to stop being so paranoid about—"

"You're going to the clinic tomorrow first thing."

"*Seriously*? Aren't you overreacting just a little?"

The condescending amusement in Max's expression put the final nail in his coffin.

"You'll stay out there until morning," Crane growled.

"Oh, c'mon . . . you *wouldn't*," Max said, lifting his head. He gave a low chuckle, but his eyes were wide and pleading. "That's just plain mean."

Crane grabbed his bottle of wine and Max's shorts and left, locking the patio door behind him. Even if Max could somehow wiggle out of his restraints, the only way off the balcony was to jump down three storeys. No, he was stuck there all night.

Serves him right. Seething, Crane went into the bedroom to strip the bed.

WEDNESDAY, NOVEMBER 8TH

Crane glanced over at the clock again. It was just past 2 a.m. Closing his eyes, he pulled the comforter up to his chin with a sigh . . . but found himself staring at the ceiling fan only a few seconds later.

"*Damn* it," he whispered.

He sat up and rubbed his face, shaking his head as he reached for the little key on the nightstand. He trudged naked through the living room to the balcony door and looked out. Max was lying on his stomach, facing away, hook and cuffs still in place. It seemed like he was asleep.

After watching Max for a moment, Crane decided to cover him up. While the days in Playa del Carmen were hot in November, the nights sometimes got chilly, and he wasn't a monster.

No. Max is the monster.

Crane snatched a blanket from the couch and quietly opened the balcony door.

Immediately, Max lifted his head. "Please," he whispered. "Please please *please*, Doc, let me in?"

Max's back and buttocks were prickled with gooseflesh, and Crane realized that though it was mild out, the bare concrete was sapping his body warmth.

He quickly bent down, unlocking the padlock, and the smell of urine reached his nose.

In the quietest, most pathetic voice, Max said, "Doc, sorry . . . I peed myself."

"Crap," Crane said, feeling ashamed of himself. "*I'm* sorry." Why was it that he always ended up apologizing to Max?

"I'm so cold," Max said, his teeth chattering. There was even a glimmer of tears in his eyes.

It was an absolutely pitiful display, and Crane's heart felt like it was being crushed in his chest. Despite the things Max had done to him, despite *everything* he'd been through, no matter how hard he tried to snuff them, Crane was helpless when it came to his feelings for the little psycho. He quickly set to work unbuckling the cuffs and collar.

The anal hook proved more of a problem. Max whimpered in pain, a high, frightened noise when Crane pulled it, so he stopped. He hadn't used lube, only spit, and things had dried to the point where removing the ball would most likely tear something inside Max. He'd made a stupid mistake.

Max groaned and turned on his side, his arms over his chest, shifting away from the piss-damp concrete.

Feeling like a complete heel, Crane swallowed thickly as he covered Max with the blanket. He scooped him up into his arms, careful not to jar the tail of the hook too much. Even so, Max let out a mewling cry and buried his face against Crane's shoulder, shivering.

Crane wasn't exceptionally strong, and Max was heavier than he looked. By the time they reached the big bathroom, Crane's arms were shaking, and he was covered in sweat even though the A/C was blasting. He had Max stand beside the shower, wrapped in the blanket, while he got the water running. Unfortunately, at this time of night, the water wasn't very warm. Unlike the newer condos on their street, their building still relied on sunshine to heat the big black water tank on the roof, and the hot water was always used up in the evening by beachgoers returning home.

"I'm sorry, this is as hot as it gets," he said and helped Max walk forward into the enclosure.

As soon as the jet of water hit Max, he cried out, his expression so miserable that if Crane didn't know him better, he'd have sworn he was about to start bawling. He stepped in behind Max and pumped some body wash into his hand.

"Okay, hold still, I'm just going to . . ." He reached down and worked a slippery finger into Max's ass, swirling it around the narrow part of the hook just before the ball.

Max keened, his hands scrabbling against the colourful Talavera tiles as Crane slowly pulled the hook free. Max grunted as the ball popped out, his legs visibly shaking, and he leaned his cheek against the shower wall for a moment, breathing heavily.

Crane washed Max all over as quickly as possible, worried about his body temperature dropping any lower, then wrapped him in one of the big thick towels.

"Come on," he said, steering Max towards the bedroom. He grabbed the remote for the room's A/C unit and turned it off before helping Max into bed. Crane piled the blankets over him and crawled under the covers, pushing the wet towel to the floor to press the length of his body against Max's.

"Oh . . . *oh*, that feels good," Max murmured, even though a shudder ran through him every few seconds.

Crane wrapped his arms around Max, holding him tight, willing his heat to transfer faster.

Soon, Max stopped trembling and turned around in Crane's embrace to face him. Their legs entwined, Max pressed his face to Crane's chest.

"I'm sorry, Doc," Max said in a tiny voice, his lips moving against Crane's skin. "I'm so sorry. Please don't do that to me again. I promise, *really* promise to listen to you next time. I swear. Just don't leave me out in the cold . . ."

Crane frowned, eyes closed, and rubbed Max's back through

the covers. "I'm sorry too. I wasn't thinking," he said. "You just pissed me off so much. But why the hell would you think I'd be anything *but* pissed off? Seriously. What were you thinking?"

"I . . . was thinking that maybe you were getting tired of me," Max replied after a short silence. "Or that you'd like a woman. An actual woman . . . not just me in a dress, you know?"

"What? Why?"

"You never seem to want me anymore. Not really."

Crane's brows rose slowly. While he knew he shouldn't put too much stock into anything Max said, he did have a point.

"Well, we've moved four times in five months. Then with this fucking ant problem . . . and the stomach bug . . ." Crane replied. "I'm just stressed out."

"You've been watching the news too much."

"I know." Crane sighed. "I can't help it."

"They're not going to find you. I promise. I'm spending very good money making sure that doesn't happen." Max ended this with a soft kiss to the side of Crane's neck.

Crane hated how much he wished there were genuine feelings behind it. Clenching his jaw, he continued stroking Max's back, surprised by the painful lump in his throat.

Crane was trapped. There was no way around it. He wasn't exactly on the Most Wanted list, but the authorities were definitely on the lookout for him. His "baffling" prison escape had been all over the news for weeks following the breakout orchestrated by Max. Even though he hadn't seen anything mentioning his name for months now, it didn't mean they were any safer . . . and he couldn't leave Max for fear of him alerting authorities, because of course he would, the little bastard.

But—and this is what galled him the most—he was also trapped by his own fucking *feelings*. Even knowing exactly how little Max cared about *anything*, Crane couldn't imagine himself leaving.

Exhaling slowly through his nose, Crane cupped one of Max's ass cheeks and gave it a gentle squeeze.

"I know you're covering our tracks," he said quietly. "Which is why bringing that girl here made me so mad."

"I know. I'm sorry. I get it. And I'm sorry I had unprotected sex with her," Max mumbled, sounding perfectly contrite. "I wasn't thinking."

"Hm."

Max pulled back, and Crane opened his eyes. The corners of Max's mouth were turned down, and he just stared at him for a few seconds. "And . . . I'm sorry if I made you jealous."

"You didn't," Crane lied. "I couldn't care less if you fucked every whore in town. I just want to know that when I'm fucking *you*, I'm not going to catch some fucking disease."

Ducking his head, Max said, "Oh, okay. All right. I'm sorry." He heaved a sigh, complete with a tiny shudder in it, then nestled back against Crane's chest. "Can you forgive me?"

The catch in Max's voice should have made Crane roll his eyes . . . but then why did he kiss the top of his head instead?

I'm in hell.

"I'll try," Crane answered and squeezed Max's backside again. Despite the time of night and all the theatrics, he was getting an erection—not that he'd fuck Max *now*, though. "As long as you go to the clinic."

They each had a forged passport and a credit card under their assumed names, but Crane couldn't help being paranoid about whether they'd stand up to scrutiny. However, the clinic for tourists was small and crowded, and the nurses and doctors were harried and overworked—he had to trust that a visit to it wouldn't blow their cover.

"Doc, I *promise* I'll go to the clinic." Max's fingers encircled the hardening shaft poking against him. "I'll even go an hour before they open just to make sure I get in." He started stroking Crane slowly.

"Good," Crane said, shutting his eyes. He let out a low groan, giving in to Max's gentle ministrations.

"Can you promise *me* something?"

"Hm?"

"Stop reading the news. Just stop it. You're driving yourself crazy, Doc."

Crane frowned. Max was right. It wasn't doing him any good scouring the Internet daily for any mention of his name. "All right." He exhaled slowly as Max's hand tightened around his cock. "I promise."

"Thank you," Max murmured, kissing up the side of Crane's neck. "And thank you for letting me come in. And for cleaning me and warming me up. I know I'm a pain in the ass."

"You are," Crane replied and gave another moan as Max cupped his balls in the other hand.

"But . . . do I make you happy? Even just a little bit?"

Max sounded so young and vulnerable that Crane's

bullshit meter didn't know what to make of it. He frowned and swallowed.

Before Crane could come up with an answer, Max said, "I know you don't believe me, but"—he rubbed his thumb over the head of Crane's dick, causing him to gasp—"you make *me* happy, Doc."

Heart melting and cock getting harder, Crane lost the battle with common sense and took hold of Max's chin to tilt his head back, seeking out his mouth.

"But aren't you afraid of catching someth—"

Crane didn't care. All he cared about were the soft lips that opened wide at his kiss, the warm tongue that surrendered to his, and the firm, sliding grasp quickly bringing him to the edge. Everything else fell away.

THREE
THE WAY TO MAKE NEW FRIENDS

THURSDAY, NOVEMBER 9TH

Carefully, Crane wrote out the cheque for next month's rent using his assumed name: Robert Montagnet. He then put the cheque in an envelope to drop off at Mr. Gómez's later, placing it next to the door alongside the hammer he'd borrowed from the landlord.

He'd finally put up the print Max had bought the week before. It was a colourful picture of a man-dog creature named Xolotl, an Aztec god and selective psychopomp, painted by a local artist. It did cheer up the place a bit. Hopefully, Mr. Gómez wouldn't give him hell for making multiple holes in the wall. His first attempt had been too high, the second too low. He'd never hung art before—Mary had always done it.

Crane grabbed a garbage bag and went to collect all the trash in the condo. There was only one bin for the whole building, so he had to make sure to get their garbage into it as soon as it went out that evening, or else the stray dogs would rip into any bag left on the curb.

Crane froze when he got to the bedroom and picked up the cheap plastic waste bin by the bed. At the very top were three used condoms. He frowned and sat down slowly on the bed, staring at the small pile of wrinkled latex. The condoms were empty, but they'd obviously been worn and not by him.

"Doc?" came Max's voice from the other room.

Crane looked up as Max walked through the door to their bedroom. He was wearing a loose white linen shirt over a pair of dark-brown shorts, and his feet were bare. There was a faint sheen of perspiration on his face, and when he took his straw fedora off, he wiped his brow with the back of his forearm, smiling at Crane. "Phew, a real scorcher out there today."

"Did you go to the clinic this morning?"

"Why in the world would I do something silly like that?" Max said, laughing as he flopped back onto the bed next to Crane, his arms and legs akimbo.

"But . . . you said . . ." Crane shook his head, the truth slowly dawning on him. "So, these are your condoms?"

Max nodded.

"The ones you wore with that girl?"

"You are correct. I did not ride that pony without a saddle, *no siree*."

"Jesus." Crane rubbed his face, weary and confused. "Well, what the *hell* was the point of lying about it? Just to piss me off?"

Max lifted his head. "I dunno. You seemed like you needed something to get your blood really *pumping*. And then later, we were having such a beautiful *tender* moment, me in your arms, all warm and loved, like a little boy safe in his papa's embrace." Max said it with a sigh, letting his head fall back onto the mattress. "Ooh, I get *verklempt* just thinking about it." He frowned and slid a hand down the front of his shorts. "Or horny. Maybe it's horny." He looked over and saw Crane's look of disbelief and shrugged, his grin coy. "Doc, *why* would I stick my dick into Gabi without wrapping it first? Who do you think I am? Jeepers . . . it's like you don't even *know* me."

Crane looked up at the ceiling and let out a slow breath.

"I'm wounded . . . really I am," Max continued, sounding amused. "And to think, I gave you such a sweet, *loving* blowie last night." Max let out a huff of breath. *"Ohhh, Doc, you make me soooo happy."*

Clenching his jaw, Crane stood. "Get up."

Max smiled wider. "Why? Where are we go—" He let out a yelp as Crane yanked him off the bed by his forearm.

"I said: get *up.*"

"All right, all right," Max replied, rubbing his arm. "Geez, you're in a mood."

"I wonder why," Crane replied, grabbing Max by the ear. He picked up the garbage bag and dragged Max out of the room and towards the front door. "Let's go."

"Where?" Max wrapped his hand around Crane's wrist, trying to dislodge him. "Ow. Fucker."

"Look at this place. It's filthy."

"Yeah? So?"

"You're going to clean it."

"What?"

"First, you're going to take out the garbage. Then you're

going to deliver the cheque to Gómez . . . and take back his hammer." He held out the bag of garbage.

"How about . . . *no*." Max laughed and turned away from Crane.

With a growl, Crane dropped the bag and grabbed Max by the back of the neck, propelling him forwards. Shoving Max hard against the door, pinning him there, Crane spoke quietly into his ear. "You're going to take the garbage out and take the goddamn rent to Gómez, or I'm going to make your night out on the balcony feel like a walk in the park."

"Jesus!" Max said, his cheek pressed hard against the wood. He glared at Crane out of the corner of his eye. "*Fine*, fuck."

"Yeah?"

"I said fine. Now let me the fuck go, asshole."

Crane clenched his jaw, tightening his grip, the urge to *crush* the life out of Max swelling like a hot wave . . . then he let go and took a step back, his chest heaving and fists at his sides.

Max turned and stared at him unblinking, his gaze cold and reptilian as he slowly lifted a hand to touch the back of his neck.

Fear like a cold, hard fist in his gut, Crane took a half step back.

I've finally gone too far.

The thought had barely taken hold before Max sighed and rolled his eyes dramatically.

"Gaaawd, you're so *tedious*. It's always 'clean *this*, pick up *that*, don't get cum on the sheets' . . . What are you? My dad?" Max snorted and shook his head, picking up the garbage bag in one hand and putting the envelope between his teeth so he could open the door with the other.

Crane watched him go, Max mumbling to himself as he dragged the garbage bag down the narrow stone steps. Then, pulse still speeding, Crane closed the door and let out a slow breath. Max had forgotten the hammer, but maybe keeping it around was a good idea. Crane let out a quiet laugh and picked it up, holding it against his chest for a moment.

You know what I hate, Doc? In a movie, when one guy hits another guy in the back of the head with a hammer, and the guy falls down dead. In real life, you'd have to keep hitting him, like with good solid swings, you know? Meanwhile, the guy is thrashing around, bleeding like a stuck pig. Who wants that? Totally inefficient. Naw, the trick to killing someone with a hammer is hitting them as hard as you can right here. Grinning like a cat, Max had reached out and tapped Crane's temple lightly with his index finger.

Crane sighed again. Even if he could bring himself to brain the little psycho . . . then what? He set down the hammer, then went to the kitchen, pouring a good three fingers of tequila into the cleanest glass on the counter.

He took a sip of the Patron Reposado with a grimace. Max loved tequila, but it had yet to grow on Crane, despite how many bottles they went through in a week. He took his glass to the lumpy couch and sat down, waiting for Max to return.

A few minutes later, the floor behind him squeaked, startling him from his thoughts. He hadn't heard the front door. Max's hands came down softly on his shoulders and squeezed.

"You hurt my neck a bit, Doc."

Crane closed his eyes—there was no anger in Max's voice, just gentle admonishment.

"I know," he said and took another tiny sip of tequila, shuddering at the taste. "I'm sorry."

"I don't know why you let yourself get so *pissed* at me. It's not good for you."

Crane shook his head, wincing as Max began massaging the knots at the base of his neck. He *was* still angry, certainly, over what had happened with the girl, but mostly he was mad at himself for being stupid enough to believe *anything* that came out of Max's mouth. For all he knew, Max hadn't been trapped out on the balcony at all—maybe *all* of it had been an act. He thought about the way Max's eyes had glimmered with tears and felt nothing but disgust for himself for *hoping*...

"Yeah, I don't know why I bother either," he replied. "It's not like you'll stop being an awful little prick."

"That's better," Max murmured, brushing the side of Crane's neck with his lips. He let out a throaty chuckle. "C'mon... call me a cunt."

"You're a cunt," Crane said, squeezing his eyes shut harder as Max's tongue found the sensitive dip behind his earlobe. He exhaled twice quickly, his pulse soaring. "You're a fucking cocksucker."

"Mmm... yes—yes, I am. But I'm *your* cocksucker, aren't I, Doc?" Max's fingers walked down the front of Crane's shirt to the growing bulge in his shorts. He licked the rim of Crane's ear as he cupped his dick through the layers of material. "You wanna fuck my mouth? Choke me? I know you want it..."

Crane licked his lips, then swallowed, wanting nothing

more than precisely what Max was offering, but decided he wouldn't give him the satisfaction. He opened his eyes and grabbed Max by the wrist, pulling his hand from his erection. Max kissed him on the side of his neck, but Crane just shifted away from him and drank more tequila. He made a face. No matter how expensive the bottle was, he always tasted notes of sidewalk dirt and cigarette butt—Max thought he was crazy.

"If you didn't go to the clinic, where the fuck have you been all day?" he asked gruffly.

Max heaved a sigh, abandoning his attempts to seduce Crane, and climbed over the back of the couch to sit next to him. "I was working, actually. Courier job."

Snorting, Crane side-eyed Max. "What? Delivering food?"

"Ha." Max took the glass away from Crane and downed the rest of the tequila in one gulp. Then, smacking his lips, he smiled. "Not quite." Then his eyes widened, and his eyebrows shot up. "Oh shit, that's right, I bought you something."

Max left the couch to rummage in his ratty old messenger bag. Curious, Crane twisted around to watch Max carry a dark-brown bottle of something to the kitchen, where he rinsed out a coffee cup. Carefully, he poured some of the liquid into the mug, then added some water from a bottle in the fridge.

"What's that?" Crane was mystified.

Grinning, Max held out the drink to Crane when he returned to the couch. "Here."

Crane accepted the mug and stared down at the contents. It smelled sweet and vaguely like maple syrup. He lifted his eyes, staring at Max. "What is it?"

"Drink it. It's not poison, silly."

"Then tell me what it is."

"Don't you trust me?"

"What do you think?"

Max's grin widened. "It won't hurt you."

Crane started tipping the mug like he was going to pour it out on the floor.

"Fine. Fine . . . it's for your *empacho, Cariño.*"

"My what?"

"You know, your tummy troubles. I bought it from that lady who does the herbs next to the bank." Max's smile was full of genuine-seeming sympathy. "I told her about your stomachache, and she said you probably have *empacho.* I'm supposed to roll an egg over your belly, but I figured you'd tell me to go to hell. But her mix is, uh, fenugreek and peppermint and nothing weird. Stuff that helps with digestion and bloating—backed by science. Swear to god. I can show you online . . ."

Crane sniffed the mug's contents again; this time, he smelled peppermint.

"It's in concentrated form, so you dilute it with water. Or tequila, I guess, if you want," Max said, lightly placing his hand on Crane's knee. "Baby, I just want you to feel better."

Scoffing, Crane shook his head. Then he took a very, very small sip. It tasted medicinal but not particularly bad. Of course, if Max wanted to poison him, he'd never see it coming, so why worry? He let out a tiny bitter chuckle before taking another sip.

Max smiled wide. "There now. You'll feel better in no time." He scooted over, then laid his head in Crane's lap, folding himself into a ball on the small sofa.

Crane sighed and stroked Max's dark curls out of habit as he drank down the gritty potion.

"Mm. That's nice," Max murmured sleepily.

Chuckling, Crane tugged softly on Max's hair, causing him to let out a little moan of happiness.

"Why are you so good to me, Doc?"

Crane's hand stilled in its caresses. How could he possibly answer that?

Turning over onto his back, Max stared up at Crane with a deep crease between his brows, but he didn't say anything. Instead, he just studied his face.

Feeling a touch uncomfortable about the scrutiny, Crane looked away, unnerved by Max's serious expression. He noticed a lizard on the far wall, tiny and bright green against the white paint. As if aware of Crane's attention, the lizard moved quickly to the left a few inches, its little claws scrabbling audibly over the hard plaster. There was something . . . *peculiar* about it. Crane blinked slowly, trying to ascertain what was wrong, and took another sip from the mug. The lizard climbed onto the painting of the Aztec god . . . and disappeared behind one of the bright geometric blooms.

"What the . . ." Crane squinted, looking for the lizard. It must have been a trick of the light. But, no—there it was, peeking out from behind the flower. "Do you see . . ." Crane thought his voice sounded strange. He glanced down at Max and saw that he was grinning wide. "There's a lizard."

"Fascinating."

"It, uh—" Crane looked for it again and found it still hiding in the painting. It waved at him. "It just waved at me."

"Oh yeah? Do tell?" Max let out a low chuckle. "Are there more?"

Suddenly, there was a lizard behind every flower. Dozens of beady little black eyes stared back at Crane. Dizzy, he shook his head, and it finally dawned on him what was happening—the cup fell from his numb grasp and landed with a loud crash on the tiled floor.

"It's drugged . . ." Crane croaked.

The flowers in the painting started to sway and grow, and the man-dog in the centre smiled menacingly at him, its square eye sockets hollow.

Crane looked away, his heart pounding. "What did she put in it?"

"*She?* No, my darling. Mrs. Ortega made up a nice mix for your tummy, that's all. I'm the one who added a little extra."

"Of course you did." Crane could hear the blood coursing through his veins. He'd never felt a drug come on so fast and so hard. And it was only getting worse. His crotch felt oddly wet, like he'd pissed himself, and the saliva in his throat felt thick as molasses. "Fuuucck." Crane began to panic as the preliminary high of the drug seemed to multiply every passing second.

"*True apothecary,*" he heard Max murmur from far away, "*thy drugs art quick.*"

Spiders were crawling up Crane's arms. His shorts were gone. Snake eggs were hatching in his guts. Max's face loomed close, his eyes bigger than apples. Crane was panting and shaking . . . sweat ran off him like rivulets of seawater. He was drowning.

"Stay with me, Doc."

"Max?"

The room was dark, and music was playing. Max had Crane's dick in his mouth.

"No . . ." Crane had tears on his face.

Max smiled, his teeth as sharp as metal spikes.

Voices. Seated on an oversized couch. The tallest couch in the world. Far below, three men and a woman were on the floor. Four bodies, twining, merging as one. Hideous creature. Skin melting into skin. The woman screamed.

"Doc?"

"No!" Crane tripped over the rug, landing hard on his chest. The pain cleared his head for a moment.

Max was bent over, and a stranger was fucking him with brutal thrusts. Crane growled and launched himself at the pair, wrestling the tall man away from Max and pinning him to the ground. The face staring up at him was his own.

"O! beware, my lord, of jealousy," said his doppelganger, laughing as he struggled to free himself. "It is the green-eyed monster which doth mock the meat it feeds on . . ."

"Doc?"

The snakes in Crane's belly writhed as the man above him shouted in his face. He bucked and screamed, freeing himself, and crawled away on all fours. But it was too late . . . the snakes were getting loose. One of them emerged from a rent in his skin, and he grabbed hold of it, pulling with all his might . . . the pain was too much.

Death claimed him, and he fell headlong into the dark.

"Doc?"

Crane cracked one eye open.

Max's face hovered above him, his expression amused. The sick, paranoid feeling in Crane had subsided, and he just felt numb. He could hear voices nearby and soft New Age music.

"Where am I?" His throat was sore, and his jaw ached.

"We're at the Mayakoba."

"*What?*" The Mayakoba was a five-star hotel not far from their condo. "How?"

"Is he okay?" The woman was topless, and her wet hair hung down to her ribs, framing a pair of pale, freckled breasts.

"Yeah, I think so."

Right above the woman's collarbone was a perfect purple oval as if someone had grabbed her hard enough that their thumb had left a bruise. It took a few seconds for Crane to realize he was staring at her—he averted his gaze, face warm, hoping that she didn't think he'd been ogling her.

"Uh . . . what happened?" he asked, trying to sit up, but Max had a hand on his chest holding him down. He realized he was lying on the floor with a pillow propped under his head, naked from the waist down. Crane put a hand over his crotch.

"Well, you suddenly decided that the condo was trying to suffocate you, so we went for a walk down La Quinta. You were out of your gourd, but all right, you know? I just followed you around for a while." He laughed, scrubbing a hand through his hair. "Baby, you were saying the craziest shit."

Crane frowned, trying to remember but coming up blank. He remembered . . . music and . . . *snakes?*

"How did we wind up here?" Crane knew he was still a bit stoned—there was odd movement in his peripheral, no matter where he looked.

"Well, you wandered over to the Kitxen because there

34

was a band playing, and that's where we met Preston and Vivian . . . then we came back here."

Crane was so confused. He tried once more to sit up, pushing Max's hand away, and nearly fell over when he leaned against the couch. Quickly grabbing the cushion to cover his nakedness, Crane tried not to think about why he wasn't wearing any pants.

"Um . . . who?"

"Wow, he really doesn't remember anything?" the woman said, her blue eyes wide.

Crane guessed this was Vivian. She sounded American. He frowned, recalling something about . . . freckled skin between his hands.

"Doesn't look like it," Max replied with a smile.

Crane turned his attention back to Max, his throat tight with equal parts anxiety and anger.

What did you do to me?

Max's grin widened—he looked like the cat who'd stolen the cream. Crane wanted nothing more than to knock the gloating expression off Max's face.

He cleared his throat. "May I have some water . . . uh, Vivian? Please?"

"Sure thing, honey." She jumped and ran to get him a glass of water.

"What the fuck did you give me?" Crane growled low, his hands itching to grab Max by the throat.

"Something brand new. It's called *la víbora* . . . and I only crushed half a pill into your tummy medicine. I can't even imagine what you would have been like on a full dose. Hoo-wee. You were something else, baby." Max leaned in to kiss him.

Crane jerked his head back.

"Aw. Don't tell me you're pissed at me? From what I could tell, you were having the time of your life. Well, right up until the point where you suddenly pounced on Preston and scared the shit out of him, then you went like, *crazy* . . . trying to pull your dick off."

"What?" Crane stared at him, sorting through the only disjointed memories he could summon.

"Yeah, we had to pin you down and force-feed you some Xanax."

Vivian reappeared with a glass. She'd thrown on a shirt—Crane wondered if she was feeling self-conscious because he couldn't remember the orgy he'd obviously participated in . . . or *had* he? They were mere snatches of memories, too filmy and abstract to hang on to.

Vivian smiled and held out the water. "Here. It's got cucumber in it."

"Um. Thank you. I'm sorry for any trouble I caused." Crane accepted the glass. "I uh . . . don't know what to say."

"Oh. You're fine." Vivian gave a light chuckle, waving his concern away. "It can happen to anyone."

At that moment, a man walked into the room wearing only a white towel around his waist. He had the kind of ruggedly handsome features that belonged in a high-end menswear catalogue, complete with artfully tousled dark hair and a furry, muscular chest.

Crane frowned, beginning to remember something about the man he didn't like.

"Hey, buddy, you feeling okay?" asked the man, coming around to rest his hand on the back of Vivian's neck. She visibly tensed at his touch, and her smile froze in place, her expression masklike. "Man, you had us all worried there for a sec."

"I'll be fine," Crane replied tersely. "Thanks for your concern."

"Do you think you'll still be up for joining us on the yacht today?"

"On the . . . yacht?" Crane looked over at Max, and Max nodded.

"Yeah, Preston and Viv invited us to go boating with them. You were really excited about it last night."

"Oh yeah. Right," Crane said, pretending to remember. "Wait, what time is it?"

Vivian looked at the little gold watch on her wrist. "Just past four." She yawned. "You've had almost three hours of sleep, but the rest of us haven't had any at all. You know, y'all can take the other bed if you want to stay . . ."

"We should be heading home." Crane pushed himself to his feet, clumsy and light-headed. Trying not to think about what Max had been up to with the attractive couple for three hours while he slept, he clutched the pillow against his groin, casting around. "Um. Where are my shorts?"

FOUR
THE MISSING TIME

FRIDAY, NOVEMBER 10TH

"You're overreacting." Max rolled over onto his belly and propped his head up, chin resting on his palms. His thick, dark brows slowly rose to meet over his nose, and his mouth quirked to one side in an indulgent grin. Crane knew most people would read only fond concern in the young man's face, but all he saw was mockery.

"*Am I?*" Crane said, his voice high with exasperation. Sitting back against the headboard, he held tight to his biceps, trembling and rocking and sweaty from the aftereffects of the drug in his system. "You literally poisoned me, you shit."

"Naw . . ." Max shook his head. "*It is only the dose which makes a thing poison,*" he said, obviously quoting something. "And, like I told you, I only gave you half. I *drugged* you—I didn't *poison* you. Gee whiz, you'd think you'd be used to it by now."

"You gave me an untested drug—"

"Untested?" Max let out a chuckle and rolled over again,

tucking his hands under his head as he stared at the ceiling. His bare skin was dark against the white sheet—the only break in his tan came from the short bathing trunks he usually wore, and even then, he was getting golden there from sunning himself nude on the balcony. "Doc, just about *everything* I've given you is 'untested.'"

Crane closed his eyes. The nausea was getting worse. He reached for the glass of water on the bedside table and took another small sip. "Where did you get it anyway?"

"My courier job."

"You're dealing drugs now?"

"No. Well, not *exactly*," Max replied. "I take things from point A to point B. I'm a courier, not a dealer. So, yeah, sometimes it's drugs, but it's also liquor, money, um . . . a cocker spaniel."

"What?" Crane opened his eyes and looked over at Max.

"Yeah, his name was Gordito."

"Not the dog. I mean, who are you working for?"

"Well . . . myself. Mostly. *Sort* of." Max glanced at Crane, his eyes heavy-lidded. "How are you feeling? Well enough for a blowjob?"

"What do you mean 'sort of'?" Crane didn't like how Max was dodging his questions.

"Not a 'sort of' blowjob . . . I mean a real drool-covered throat-pounder," Max replied, reaching up to grab the sheet covering Crane's lap. He tugged, but Crane clutched hard at the sheet.

"Stop it." He winced as the motion caused his head to throb harder. He finished his water and set the glass aside, wondering if he'd manage to keep from throwing up this time. "Leave me alone."

"Okay. Sorry, Doc. Do you want me to get you anything?"

"Yes. My dignity," Crane muttered as he leaned his head back on the hard wooden bedstead. *What dignity?*

The mattress jiggled and squeaked as Max moved around. When Crane looked over, he saw Max had sat up to face him. He seemed honestly bemused.

"Aw, Doc, you're really beat up about last night, ain'tcha? Well, trust me, you don't need to be ashamed of anything. You were having a great time, and people found you sort of charming. Much better than your average drunk tourist, for sure. I don't know . . . you seemed so happy. Happier than I've seen you in a while. You really let loose for once."

"Yeah, and wound up in a fucking orgy." Crane rubbed his face, grimacing.

"What do you mean?"

"With that couple. Vivian and Preston."

"Is *that* what you think happened?" Max replied with obvious growing amusement. "Wow." He slapped both knees, the sound sharp enough to make Crane wince.

He frowned. "Isn't it?"

"Uh . . . noooo." Max's grin was crooked. "And besides, that wouldn't be an *orgy*. That's a foursome, or group sex. Though . . . I wonder what the cut-off is before it becomes an orgy. Six? Is there a consensus? And what's the real difference between an orgy and a gangba—"

"Why was she half-naked?" Crane asked impatiently.

"Oh. She had just taken a shower, is all. *Duh.*" When Crane didn't reply, Max gestured vaguely and said, "I told her we were gay, and you know, she's one of those 'Eeeeeeeeeee! The gays are so cah-*yoot*, ohmigod' types who like to show off their tits because we're not supposed to have any interest."

Crane's doubt must have been abundantly clear because Max shrugged.

"It's a thing. Trust me." His cheeks dimpled, and he cocked his head. "Do you want me to tell them we're interested? I'm sure they'd be up for it. We could say we were wanting to experim—"

"No."

"Fine, fine. Suit yourself." After a moment, Max sighed. He reached out towards Crane and rested his hand on the mattress, palm up like he wanted him to take it.

Staring at Max's hand on the sheet, Crane shook his head. "You're not forgiven."

"What can I do to make you forgive me?"

"I don't know."

"Well, I'll think of something." Max smiled gently. "I'll make it up to you for last night . . . and for what's going to happen today." His giggle was mischievous.

Crane looked up, his pulse kicking up in response to Max's words. "What?"

The whites of Max's eyes shimmered, the tiny reflections of light multiplying as Crane watched on in horror.

"No."

The whine of the A/C in the background took on a sinister note.

"I'm afraid so, Doc."

Crane glanced back down at Max's hand. It was dry and brittle against the white sheets, skin flaking off like a mummy's desiccated claw . . . then when Max flexed his fingers, the hand became a colossal spider. Crane cried out when it jumped to its feet and skittered towards his knee. He bashed his head on the headboard as he tried to evade the spider, but he barely felt it.

"No. God, no . . ." Crane said, his tongue fumbling against the back of his teeth. His saliva was thick, like syrup in his throat. He gagged and coughed, scrabbling at his neck with numb fingers. He looked over at his glass of water—he'd poured it himself . . . *hadn't* he?

"How?" he managed. "Why?"

"You said it yourself—*la víbora* is untested, *non*? So, *you're* field testing it, lucky duck! And, this time, I gave you a full dose," Max said, leaning towards Crane, his face full of shifting shadows and light.

Crane closed his eyes, his heart racing. Something turned over in his stomach. He had the sudden impression of a giant snake curled up in his guts, just beginning to awaken.

"This should be fun. Now, don't worry, *mi amor*. I'll take good care of youuuuuuuuu . . ."

Crane's blood was teeming with tiny worms. Terrified, he started to scream.

○

SUNDAY, NOVEMBER 12TH

Groaning, Crane slowly came awake. He was cold and uncomfortable, his hips and knees aching and his throat raw. When he opened his eyes, he stared around in confusion. It took him a minute to realize where he was.

Crane winced and grunted, grabbing the side of the bathtub with a throbbing hand, and tried to pull himself up. However, one of his legs was hooked over the side of the tub, and the other was jammed awkwardly against the tiled wall so he couldn't sit.

Something floppy and cold slid in his lap with his motions —he fished around under the thin blanket that partially covered him and came up with a baggie filled with water.

What the hell?

Across the bathroom, his clothing hung on the clothesline in the shower stall. He lowered his head back onto the pillow, breathing heavily from the effort of moving around and lay there, confused, his head full of cotton and a yawning chasm in his memory.

Max walked into the bathroom. "Oh, good. I thought I heard you." He sat on the edge of the tub. Smiling down at him, he asked, "How are you feeling this time?"

"*This* time?" rasped Crane, his eyes watering.

"I guess you weren't *quite* awake the last time." He held out his hand.

Something about the sight of Max's hand, palm up, filled Crane with dread, and he shook his head.

"Silly, I'm trying to help you out of the tub," Max said impatiently and grabbed Crane's wrist. "Come on . . . alley-oop, Doc."

Relenting, Crane let himself be pulled to sitting, then, with Max's assistance, he untangled his legs and managed to get to his feet. He was amazed by how weak he felt. With an arm over Max's shoulders, he made it to the bed and sunk down on the squeaky mattress. He lay back against the propped pillows in silent bewilderment as Max covered him to the waist with a cool, crisply clean sheet.

"I'll be right back."

Crane closed his eyes. He felt like he'd just woken from a

nightmare—anxious, confused . . . and something else. Guilty? Ashamed? As if he'd done something wrong? No, that wasn't quite right.

"Here."

Looking up, Crane saw Max was holding out a glass full of purple liquid.

"No," he whispered. Max had drugged him. *That* he remembered.

Max chuckled and sat down. "It's that juice from down the street," he said, holding it out to Crane.

"Drugs . . ."

"No drugs. Just carrots, strawberries, and blueberries. And I got them to put honey in it, just like you like it."

"No."

"Don't be a baby. You need your antioxidants. I promise . . . no funny business."

Crane started laughing, an ugly hoarse sound, helpless tears springing to his eyes.

Max stared at him, his smile fading. With a frown, he held out the glass again.

This time Crane took it like a good boy and didn't even question it when Max put two pills in his other hand, explaining they were tryptophan and *Mucuna pruriens* to help him recover.

Crane obediently popped the pills into his mouth and downed half the glass of juice without hesitation. Max could have told him they were cyanide pills, and he would have done the same.

What did it matter anymore?

FIVE
THE THREAT AND THE CONFESSION

WEDNESDAY, NOVEMBER 15TH

Crane stared at the tiny blue triangles in the hand-painted border that went across the far wall. They were all imperfect, uneven, and the brushstrokes noticeable even without his glasses. Sometimes they overlapped the bigger yellow triangles, creating a liminal green area. Above his head, the A/C unit hummed.

It had been three days since he had woken up naked and confused in the bathtub. Three days since Max had drugged him with a powerful narcotic that had wiped more than forty-eight hours from his memory. Hours where he had evidently pissed and shit himself, his clothes already sodden with sweat and vomit. Hours where he had been entirely at Max's mercy.

Hours he would never get back.

Crane closed his eyes, his stomach knotted from hunger and anxiety. Earlier, when Max had tried to tell him exactly what had happened, he'd stopped him. Honestly, Crane was glad he couldn't remember any of it. He sighed and turned over onto his back, one hand scratching at the hair on his belly, then lower down, beneath his boxers, testing. The reason he'd had a baggie of ice resting on his crotch was to help with the swelling and the bruises—self-inflicted, according to Max. Crane wondered why he kept trying to emasculate himself every time Max drugged him.

A soft tread at the threshold told him Max was there, but he didn't turn, just stared at the cracks in the ceiling plaster.

"I'm going out. I left a sandwich in the fridge for you," Max said in a quiet voice. "I won't be back until after dark. Call me if there's anything, okay?"

Crane didn't answer.

"Doc?" Max waited a few seconds, then sighed audibly. "Okay, then. I'll see you later."

He waited until he heard the lock turning in the front door, then sat up, his bladder full. Dizzy, he made his way to the bathroom and sat down on the john, too unsteady to piss standing up. He'd eaten here and there, but sleeping for twenty hours a day was tiring, ironically, so he kept winding up back in bed.

He rubbed his face, his stubble thick and skin oily against his palms, and groaned quietly as he drained his bladder. He had no idea what time it was. Max had just said he'd be back after dark . . . did that mean it was afternoon? Crane sighed and stood, pulling up his boxers, then flushed the toilet as he peered at himself in the bathroom mirror. With his hair wild, eyes deeply shadowed, and gaunt face unshaven, he barely recognized himself.

"Christ, you look like the Unabomber," he muttered to his reflection as he pulled his lower eyelid down to inspect his bloodshot eye.

Crane's stomach chose right then to rumble again, and he remembered that Max had said something about a sandwich. A sandwich sounded nice . . . he just hoped it wasn't drugged. With a raspy, sad little chuckle, he left the bathroom in search of food.

The sandwich was actually a *torta*, a thick stack of ingredients between two halves of a *telera* roll, and Max had left a note propped up next to it in the fridge with *bon appétit* scrawled in a lazy hand, punctuated by a smiley face. With a scowl, Crane crumpled the note and tossed it in the garbage. Sitting on the couch, he lifted the top off the *torta*, frowning at the lettuce and grilled poblanos. Could he even tell if there was something wrong with it? Probably not.

With a sigh, he replaced the bread and picked up the *torta*, bracing himself. The first bite was an incredible explosion of flavour that had him closing his eyes in pleasure as he chewed. There was avocado, *cotija*, something pickled, the crunch of fresh red onions, salsa verde . . . cilantro . . . he opened his eyes to look at the *torta* again, trying to identify the meat he was chewing. He smiled when it came to him—pan-seared, breaded pork. He shook his head and took another bite. When Max was motivated to cook, something that rarely happened, he always impressed.

The boy had real talent . . . which was why his mother and stepfather thought he was in Paris studying at Le Cordon Bleu for his Grand Diplôme. Max had made a deal with a student at the institute to cover for him—in return for Max funding the course, the culinary student was dutifully updating Max's Facebook with pictures of Paris and the school, as well as Max's various Parisian apartments, which were really in Mexico but artfully doctored to include the Paris skyline whenever a window was visible.

This meant Max's absence was covered for the nine months of the gastronomy programme, after which he would undoubtedly find some other excuse for why he wasn't in Montréal. So far, the hardest thing was keeping his mother from going to Paris to visit him.

Crane thumped his chest, dislodging a burp, and set aside his plate on the couch, sitting back to wait and see whether some drug was going to take over his system again. After a few minutes, all he felt was sated and no longer light-headed. Maybe he was in the clear.

He looked around, wondering what to do. It was midafternoon, as it turned out, which meant he was on his own for a few hours. While he didn't feel like returning to bed, he wasn't quite up for leaving the condo either.

Glancing over, he saw Max had left his laptop behind—it sat open on the tiny dining table.

Crane smiled. With no TV in the condo, they relied on Max's MacBook for entertainment. The internet connection at the condo was dead slow most of the time, but at least a hundred movies were scattered on Max's numerous external hard drives. He'd been meaning to rewatch *Calvary* and remembered seeing it on one of them.

He got up, reaching for his plate to put it away, and frowned at the empty spot on the couch.

That's weird.

Confused, he went to the kitchen, and there was his plate sitting on the kitchen counter. Maybe he was drugged after all . . . but it didn't *feel* like it. Chalking up his absentmindedness to fatigue and the aftereffects of a full dose of *la víbora*, he shrugged to himself and went to fetch his glasses from the bedside table.

Crane went back to the laptop and touched the trackpad to wake the screen. He frowned as it brightened instantly— usually, when the computer woke up, he was presented with a screen where he could put in his own username and password. However, this time the chaos of Max's desktop greeted him. Did that mean Max was still logged in?

He picked up the laptop and took it back to the couch, wondering what he should do. How did he get the thing to switch to his user? Crane knew almost nothing about computers.

Max had set up an account on his laptop for Crane to use with only the most relevant icons, like the orange fox hugging the world that was labelled "Look, it's the Internet!" and the postage stamp with a bird on it labelled "This is email, dummy."

He tried closing the laptop cover and waiting a few seconds before opening it again, but that didn't work. He was still logged into Max's account.

Annoyed, Crane scanned the clutter of blue folders labelled things like "rapebot 3D render1 final final2 REALfinalomg" and "randos – tentacles, scales, and dogdicks," looking for a way to log out. Then he saw it—right in the middle of the mess was a folder labelled "Mary."

Crane licked his lips and swallowed, rubbing a hand over his mouth. Mary? *His* Mary?

Who else would it be, Doc?

His finger slid over the trackpad, the little black arrow skimming along the screen to come to rest on the blue folder.

What good would come of opening it, even just to peek at what was inside?

You know you want to.

Disconcerted, he closed the laptop and pushed it to the other side of the couch.

Stupid.

He stood and went back to the kitchen to tackle the stack of dishes. The folder was probably just full of her financial records and stuff—research Max had done to find out everything about her. He kept a file on everyone, supposedly.

Yeah, that's all it is.

Crane scrubbed hard at the pan Max had used to cook the breaded pork in, cursing him for leaving him to clean up the mess.

Maybe there are emails in that folder. Ones they wrote to each other.

Max had sought her out in his guise of poor little Édouard Duvernay—Max's real name but definitely not his real identity—a victim of Dennis Crane's fictional torture. Yeah, *surely* Max and Mary had corresponded over email . . .

Why don't you go find out? said the voice of his twisted conscience. *Don't you want to read what they said about you?*

Crane ground his teeth together, breathing quickly through his nose as he wiped down the countertop.

No. I don't care. Whatever it is, it's bound to be perverse, he thought.

But how *perverse?* It was like a dare.

Pouring himself a finger of tequila, Crane splashed some orange juice into the glass before returning to the couch. He looked over at the laptop. It was covered in layers and layers of stickers. From the side, a cross-section of the cover would probably look like the striations of sedimentary rock or tree rings, a physical manifestation of time. He lifted his glass, fixing his gaze on the most prominent sticker on the laptop cover, a big yellow winking smiley face.

"Fuck you," he whispered to it. He downed his drink in one swallow, grimaced, then seated the laptop squarely on his knees. Of *course*, he would look in the folder.

The laptop came awake as he opened the cover, and he half expected it to show him the login screen, just to fuck with him, but no—the folder with his ex-wife's name on it was right there, centre stage.

This time he didn't hesitate. He double-clicked on the blue folder, and it opened a new window with a list of files ending in .mp4. They were videos, but none had descriptive titles, just a series of sequential numbers, perhaps relating to the order they had been taken in.

Taking a deep breath, he double-clicked on the first one and instantly regretted it.

Mary smiled at the camera and then covered her mouth as she giggled, suddenly shy. She was sitting in the bedroom of the house they had owned. Crane recognized the landscape painting on the wall behind her—it had hung above their bed.

"I feel stupid," Mary whispered.

"Why? Am I making you feel stupid?" came Max's voice from behind the camera.

Clenching his jaw, Crane gripped the sides of the laptop.

"No! No . . . it's not that I just—" Mary shrugged and raked her fingers through her dark-brown curls, pushing her hair over her shoulder. "I don't do this sort of thing usually."

"What sort of thing? What are we doing?" Max sounded

like he was smiling. "We're not *doing* anything . . . I'm just interviewing you."

You little fucker.

Mary laughed again, the dimples deep in her soft, round cheeks and her teeth very white as she threw her head back. Then she covered her eyes, shaking her head. When she looked into the camera again, she was blushing.

You goddamn motherfucking little cocksucker.

"Ready?" asked Max.

Mary grinned wide, cleared her throat, and nodded, straightening her shoulders.

"All right. How old are you, Mary?"

She lifted her gaze from the camera's eye, looking past it to the young man recording her. "You should never ask a woman her age, don't you know that?"

"Sorry, I thought I would start simple. Want me to guess?" Max asked. "I . . . guess . . . twenty-five?"

Mary let out a peal of laughter. "What! Don't be ridiculous."

"Sorry . . . twenty . . . *two?*"

Mary made a face. "Stop it."

"What?"

"I'm probably old enough to be your mother."

"Nuh-uh. No way."

Her mouth quirked to the side, appraising him. "How old are *you*, anyway?"

"Old enough," Max replied with a chuckle. "All right . . . if you're not going to tell me, I'm going to keep guessing."

"Fine," Mary said with a smirk. She looked directly into the camera. "I'm thirty-nine."

"I don't believe you."

"Believe what you want. I'll be forty next month." She laughed again. "You make me feel like a dirty old woman."

Crane exhaled through clenched teeth. That meant the video had been taken in March, four months into his incarceration, and evidently, they'd known each other for longer, given how they were in the bedroom together. He knew Max had fucked his wife but hadn't *really* believed it. He put the arrow on the moving dot below the video in the player and dragged it to the right about an inch.

"—think about when you masturbate?"

Wow, that escalated quickly. Crane scowled.

Mary's cheeks were dark pink, and she wouldn't look at the camera. "The usual . . . I don't know. I don't do that very often."

"Why not?"

"I don't know."

"Am I making you uncomfortable?"

Nodding, Mary looked at the young man behind the camera. "I sort of like it, though," she confessed quietly.

"Do you?" It was obvious Max was amused, even though he kept his voice low and intimate. "Good . . . that's why I'm doing this. I want to know *exactly* what you like. I want to make you feel good."

Damn you fucking goddamn motherfucking . . .

"You're good at doing that, Eddie."

The fondness in Mary's flirtatious grin made Crane want to throw up, but he gritted his teeth and forced himself to watch the rest of the video. Other than the revelation that she'd cheated on him once in high school, there was nothing shocking, which was why he was so unprepared when he opened the second video file.

He gaped at the moving image on the screen for all of three seconds before he hit the stop button. In full, lurid detail was a close-up of his wife's pussy—*unmistakably* hers—being penetrated by a very familiar cock.

There. *There* was the proof, right there in front of his fucking face, that Max had fucked his wife. He hit play and watched the cock piston in and out of Mary's wet hole. She was moaning like it was the best thing she'd ever had.

"You never sounded like that with me," Crane said in a hoarse voice. "And you fuck *him* and sound like a porn star."

The camera panned back a little to show Mary on the bed, her legs spread wide as she played with her nipples, whimpering and groaning in pleasure with every deep plunge of Max's cock. Then the camera went further upwards as Max held it above his head. He stared directly up into it, his grin sly, and he winked as he thrust and thrust and thrust . . .

Crane was livid.

He was also rock-hard.

He watched to the end of the video and lifted the laptop off his knees and onto the couch to pull his boxers down. Then, with his hand around his cock, he double-clicked the next movie.

Crane barely registered it when the door to the condo opened a while later. He was three-quarters of the way through the files and had reached the point where Max had finally convinced Mary to let him fuck her in the ass. She was nervous, that much was obvious. Max had accidentally sodomized her a few files back, and she was worried about the pain. At this point, Crane *wanted* it to hurt her. The one time he'd brought up anal sex, she threatened to make him sleep on the couch if he dared ask again.

His cock drooled out another long drip of precum as he stroked himself, the video shifting perspectives so that he could watch her asshole being fingered from up close.

Max walked into the living room and, after watching Crane for a moment, pulled his T-shirt over his head and stepped out of his shorts.

Then, without a word, he spat onto his fingers, reached behind himself, and crawled onto the couch to straddle Crane's lap. Crane pushed the laptop out of the way of Max's knee but didn't close it, eyes on the screen as Max sank down slowly onto his cock. Once Crane was balls-deep inside him, Max began to move, fucking Crane languidly at first but then faster when Crane let out a soft groan.

Mary was whimpering in pain, shoving back at Max's thigh, trying to keep him from going any deeper. Crane panted a few breaths and grabbed Max by the hips, slowing him. Then he forced Max to move at the same pace as on the video.

It didn't take long after that.

Crane let out a strangled cry as he climaxed, and even before the last blast of cum had left his balls, he burst into helpless tears.

Max moaned as he kept riding Crane's cock for a few seconds longer, but when Crane began shuddering and gasping through his sobs, Max opened his eyes and stopped moving.

Dark brows meeting over his nose, he stared down at Crane.

"What's wrong?" he asked, his expression growing more bewildered.

Shaking his head, Crane shoved weakly at Max, his breath hiccupping in his chest. When he wouldn't move, Crane slapped the laptop shut, ending Mary's gasps and squeals of protest.

"I—I ca—can't," Crane said, tears streaming down his face. "I can't do this."

"You just *did*, from the sounds of it." Max smirked.

When Crane shook his head again, Max rose on his knees, and Crane's semi-limp dick slid out of him, plopping down onto his stomach with a wet little *slap*. He stood, watching Crane weep.

"Doc, what's *wrong*?"

Closing his eyes, Crane turned away. He bowed his head, arms around himself, and continued to bawl until his chest hair was soaked, and he was utterly exhausted—Max didn't say a word the whole time.

Finally, Crane wiped his nose on the back of his wrist, sighed, and opened his eyes. To his surprise, Max was still there, motionless as a statue and staring at him with a deep furrow in his brow.

"Doc?" Max said quietly. "What the hell was that?"

"I'm done." Crane shrugged. "I can't do this anymore."

"What do you mean?" asked Max, an apprehensive note in his voice.

"I mean, I'm done. I'm going to turn myself in," Crane said tiredly. He felt calm now, like the tears had washed away his fears. "Or, if your plan was to kill me all along, you might as well do it now. I won't struggle." He shrugged, looking out at the blue sky beyond the patio door.

"You can't mean that."

"I can, and I do. I'm done. You win. I can't fight anymore. I don't care. I just . . ." Crane exhaled slowly and rubbed his face—his drying tears had made his cheeks tacky. "I just want this to end. I can't live like this. I don't want to."

"Oh, c'mon, Doc. Knock it off," Max said with a nervous-sounding laugh. "I'm not going to kill you . . . *geez louise.*"

"I just want the torture to stop."

"Torture? Dramatic, much?" Max let out another laugh, even more uncertain than the last. "I was just playing around, Doc . . . you know that, right?"

"I'm done." Crane closed his eyes again and leaned his head back on the couch. He felt like he could sleep for a week straight. The couch sank down next to him—he could smell the sunscreen on Max's skin.

"Doc? C'mon . . . snap out of it. You're just hungry or something. We can go down to the—"

"I'm done," Crane repeated. "It's done." He'd call the cops today . . . maybe not the local cops though. He had no idea if the stereotype of Mexican jails had any truth to it, but he didn't want to find out. Crane was at the end of his rope, but that didn't mean he was a masochist. He'd go back to Québec and do his time there.

"You *want* to go to jail?"

"Anything is better than being here with you."

"I . . . thought you loved me."

Crane let out a bitter little laugh but didn't reply.

After a few seconds of silence, Max said, "I won't let you."

Crane looked over at him. The muscles in his jaw were twitching, and his eyes were hard, but he was visibly pale.

"What are you going to do? Tie me up?" Crane said.

"If I have to."

"And watch me twenty-four hours a day?"

"Doc, be reasonable. C'mon, you won't really turn yourself in, will you?" Max chewed on the corner of his lip, the challenge in his gaze had turned to apprehension again. "Please don't, Dennis . . ."

The sound of his name on Max's lips always annoyed him, now even more because he was obviously trying to manipulate him like usual.

"Listen to me," Crane said. "I would rather be *anywhere* in the world than spend one more fucking hour with you and your sick games. I would rather spend the rest of my life rotting in jail as someone's 'wife.' I'd welcome it *gladly* if it meant I never had to see your face again. You know what, I would rather *die* than stay here with *you*."

As soon as Crane said it, he knew he didn't really mean it.

However, the effect his words had on Max was immediate.

The young man looked away, but not before Crane saw his expression crumple. He stood and stared at his feet, his naked body rigid and hands balled at his side as he panted a few short breaths. If he was playing at getting himself under control, it was pretty convincing.

Crane frowned.

"Please stay." Max's voice was small and scared. "Please reconsider."

"No."

Max cast about, his gaze shifting rapidly like he was searching for an answer in the air around him. If Crane didn't know any better, he would have said Max was panicking.

Then Max's shoulders slumped, and he turned to face

Crane, but he didn't meet his eyes. "All right . . . go. But don't turn yourself in. I'll give you money. You've got your passport . . . you can travel and live anywhere you want. And I'll set up an email address that you can use to reach me, any time, if ever there's anything—and I mean *anything*—that you need . . . I'll take care of it. No questions asked. And . . . I'll do it in a way that you don't ever have to see me. Ever. Promise."

Crane's frown deepened, and he felt a niggling of doubt.

"Yeah, *right*. I'll get myself set up somewhere and one day, out of the blue, I'll wake up to you in my bed . . . wearing crotchless panties or something."

Max snorted, but his smirk had no life in it. "No."

Crane started feeling something akin to hope. He sat up. "You'll just let me go. That's it?"

"That's it."

"I can leave tonight?"

"That's your prerogative," Max said quietly. He lifted his eyes and met Crane's gaze. "I'm sorry for everything."

"No, you're not." It was Crane's standard reply to Max's apologies. He found himself smiling like he did when his admonishments were meant only to tease, but Max just sat down slowly at the table, his expression numb.

Crane wasn't sure what reaction he'd been expecting, but this wasn't it. The hope he'd felt just a few seconds earlier was tempered with uncertainty. He ran a hand through his hair, his eyes on Max.

C'mon, Doc . . . are you really *going to leave?* whispered the voice in his head.

"I'll pack my things today and leave tomorrow," he said. It felt like an empty threat, just to get Max to say something, and he very nearly added a childish "I mean it."

Max just nodded.

Crane glanced down at his drying, cum-crusted cock, at a loss for words. He should have been relieved, but all he felt was confused. If this were happening to one of his patients, he would have attributed the hesitation to Stockholm syndrome . . . but this was more than that, wasn't it?

He rubbed his palms on his thighs, mentally preparing himself to stand and, what? Pack? Make plans to live as an expat . . . somewhere? He'd never been good at travelling. Where would he go? What would he do?

You could just say you didn't mean it, his conscience pointed out.

But I did mean it . . .

"I lied to you," Max said softly into the tense silence.

Crane let out a bark of laughter. "Water is wet; the sky is blue . . . tell me something I *don't* know." He cleared his throat. "So, you weren't planning on letting me go after all?" It mortified him how absolutely relieved he felt about that.

Max glanced over at him, his brow creased and his mouth set in a hard line. "I didn't mean just *now*. You can go if you fucking want. I mean . . . when we first met. I lied to you."

Cocking his head, Crane stared at Max. "I know that."

"No. You don't," Max replied, maintaining eye contact for a few silent seconds before sighing and looking away again. "I told you there was no history of trauma. I lied."

Crane was taken aback for a moment before he narrowed his eyes, scrutinizing Max. "O . . . kay," he said, wondering where he was going with this.

Max's gaze flicked back to him, his expression guarded. "If I tell you something real about me—about my past—will you stay?"

Crane frowned. "Go on."

Max turned slightly in his seat so he was facing Crane, and Crane was taken back to the first time Max had sat down across from him in therapy. Crane swallowed, his face growing warm as he remembered the first time the young man had crawled forward on his hands and knees to—

"My father—my real father's name is Maurice Richard."

"The hockey player?" Crane knew nothing about sports, but that was a name he recognized.

"It's a common name in Québec. But, no, my father *was* an accountant."

"*Was?* What is he doing now?"

"Well, he's been sitting in a cell." Max shook his head and looked up at the ceiling. "He got fifteen fucking years . . . what a joke."

"What did he do?" Crane felt like he should have a notebook at hand.

Max locked eyes with Crane, his jaw jutting forward. "I want doctor-patient confidentiality . . . I *mean* it. If I *ever* find out you've told *anyone*, I'd be royally pissed . . . *Capisce?*"

"Of course. I promise," Crane replied, though it was farcical to frame their twisted relationship as professional in any way. "What happened?"

Max took a deep breath and answered. "My father's serving a fifteen-year sentence for manufacturing and distributing child pornography."

"Oh." Crane frowned, leaning forward. "Wait. Does that mean . . . *you* . . . were the . . .?"

"Star of his movies?" Max laughed, an ugly little sound as he looked away. "Yeah. I was his *star*. Good thing I didn't have siblings, eh? I'm not sure I could have competed with a sister."

Crane didn't know what to say. It just seemed too . . . *convenient* for the information to come out now, right when Max stood to lose his favourite plaything.

Max scowled at the doubt obviously written on Crane's face.

"What? Don't believe me?" he said. "I don't know when it first started, but I remember him giving me one hell of a 'surprise' for my birthday. I thought I was getting the stuffed toy cheetah I saw at the store. Instead, he told me I was old enough to start playing a new game." Max wiped his mouth with the back of his hand, sitting up straight. He gave a strange, hoarse little giggle, closing his eyes. "Happy birthday to me."

Crane wanted to call bullshit . . . but maybe it *would* explain a lot about Max and his obsession over control, not to mention his desire to twist every sex act into one of deviance.

No. Don't do that. Don't fall for it. It's just another lie to keep you here. But . . . what if . . .

"How long did it go on?"

"Too long." Max shook his head. "Someone *finally* recognized the décor of the motel where he liked to shoot his little videos. Fucking pervert."

"I don't . . . um . . ." Crane floundered, trying to remember his training.

"You don't believe me?" Max's laugh was shrill as he stood up and grabbed the laptop from the couch. He dropped the cold slab of metal in Crane's lap.

Crane stared up at him, rendered speechless by the raw anger in Max's voice and the wet shimmer in his eyes. "Go on . . . open that up. Launch the VPN and open the Tor browser. Won't take more than a few keywords to find some videos of me, Doc . . . they're all still online." Max wiped his nose on his wrist, tears pouring down his cheeks, his voice rough and wavering as he spoke. "*Do it.* C'mon, it'll be fun . . . we'll watch them together—I've seen them all a hundred times."

What if it *wasn't* an act? Crane frowned. It *felt* real . . .

"I don't—" Crane started again, his guts beginning to knot.

What if Max was *actually* giving him a glimpse behind the mask? What if this was his first *real* chance to connect with the young man who had set his world on fire in more ways than one? He'd blow that chance by doubting Max, that was for sure. He pressed his lips together, trying to think of what to say.

"Do you *know* what that sort of shit does to a person's sense of control? No, why *should* you? You're a *shitty* psychologist, Doc. The *worst*. You nuh-know that?" Max was crying hard now, his whole body trembling as he held himself rigid. "Y-you wanted to know why I'm th-the way I am . . . w-well, now you do." He stared a challenge at Crane, his breath hitching in his chest.

"Where . . . was your mother? Did you tell her?" Crane asked quietly.

"What? You think my mother didn't *know*? She knew the whole time it was going on and did nothing." He stared at Crane, "Sh-she did *nothing*." Max's anger seemed to break with those words, and he covered his face as he sobbed freely.

Startled, Crane shoved the laptop aside and rose off the couch, enveloping Max in his arms. He thought Max would push him away for a second, but then he suddenly sagged into his embrace. The two of them wound up on the couch in a tangle, Max crying his heart out while Crane held on tight, trying to offer words of comfort.

Yes, sexual abuse in Max's childhood would undoubtedly explain his need to manipulate and control others, especially older men like himself.

Crane remembered what Max's mother had said the night he'd met her: *Pumpkin, you do like them older, don't you?* Had there been a knowing smile on her lips?

What kind of a mother stands by while her child is being molested? A complicit one. Crane hugged Max harder. Still . . . he felt that soft, niggling doubt again. Hadn't he just, *moments* ago, cried himself out sitting in the *very same* spot? Was Max really opening up, or was he putting on a show of emotional mimicry to put Crane's subconscious at ease and trick it into believing they shared a real bond?

Well, don't *we, Doc?*

Finally, Max's crying jag seemed to lose steam, and he just sniffled quietly as he lay against Crane's chest.

"You know, he did give me a stuffed teddy bear afterwards, but I wanted a cheetah. A *cheetah.* I found my mom's sewing scissors, and I cut that bear up." Max exhaled a shuddery breath. "Fucking asshole couldn't even remember what I wanted for my birthday."

Crane closed his eyes at the pain in the troubled young man's voice and stroked his back. "I'm sorry," he whispered. "No one should go through that."

When Max twitched and let out a sigh a few minutes later, Crane realized he'd fallen asleep. He sat there quietly as Max slept in his arms, pensive. It all kept coming back to one question: why should he believe Max *now?*

Yes, early sexual trauma, paired with a single mother—

from what Crane remembered, Évangéline had raised Max on her own for years before marrying Marc Ouimet—those were cornerstones of later antisocial behaviour, weren't they? A lonely childhood was another. Max was an only child . . . that was lonely, wasn't it? It certainly had been for Crane.

Then there was bedwetting, fire starting, and animal cruelty. He knew Max wasn't guilty of the latter as a child, but he wondered about the others.

Crane frowned. Was he conflating the root causes of ASPD with the makings of a serial killer? He couldn't remember. He sighed. Max was right—he *was* a shitty psychologist. He was a better pencil-pusher than headshrinker, that was for sure—if he hadn't quit working at the bank to get his psychology degree, he would have been a manager by now. And he and Max would never have met . . .

Max moaned in his sleep. Crane looked down, smoothing Max's brown curls, and thought about the difference between love and hate. *Was* there one?

Slowly, he slid the laptop closer and lifted the cover. After some confusion, he found the fox web browser in the pop-up menu thing at the bottom of the screen and clicked it to start the Internet. Hunting and pecking with one finger, pausing when Max made a noise, he typed out Max's father's name. The first link brought him to the hockey player's page on Wikipedia, but he clicked on *For other uses, see Maurice Richard (disambiguation)* at the top.

There were a few Maurice Richards: a few politicians, a filmmaker, and there, at the bottom: *Maurice Richard (Canadian), convicted rapist.* He clicked on the link and read through the entry. It was short and to the point, supporting Max's story even though the victim's identity was withheld for legal reasons. It also didn't mention Évangéline by name, but from what Max had explained, Wikipedia could somehow be edited. Crane didn't know how that worked but guessed Marc Ouimet paid his PR team well to keep him free from his wife's scandal. No doubt he could afford to pay to censor the entry.

Crane closed the Internet window and then shut the laptop.

"Max . . ." he whispered, shaking him gently. "Hey."

"Mm?"

"Let's go to bed."

"Y're staying?" Max mumbled, rubbing sleepily at his face as he pulled away, blinking up at Crane.

"Of course, I'm staying." Crane smiled. "Where would I go?"

SIX
THE EXCURSION WITH THE AMERICANS

SUNDAY, NOVEMBER 19TH

Crane sighed inwardly and nodded, smiling politely at Preston as the man went on and on about equity and tax loopholes. A trust fund baby, Preston was obviously out of touch with reality—at least Vivian had worked at her father's marketing agency before handsome, impossibly rich Preston had swept her off her feet. She was rather more interesting to talk to, but she was off giving Max a tour of the 160-foot yacht.

Blinking, Crane focused on Preston, realizing he'd been asked a question.

"I'm sorry?"

"I said do you want another?" Preston pointed to Crane's glass.

They'd been drinking strawberry and mango margaritas all afternoon, and Crane was sick of the sweetness.

"Uhh . . ." Crane replied, looking at the ice in the bottom of his glass.

"Something different? I've got a Petrus Pomerol 2004 I'd love to crack open."

"Um. Do you have any whiskey?"

"Whiskey! Of course, I have whiskey. Scotch? Irish? Japanese? Hang on; I'll get Néstor to tell us what's in the bar." Preston waved to the white-clad crewmember who stood nearby. "Get Néstor, will ya?"

The man nodded and left, and Preston turned back to Crane. "A whiskey man, huh? I didn't figure you for a whiskey man." Preston grinned wide.

"No?" Crane asked, wishing Max and Vivian would come back from their tour.

"I thought y'all just liked, you know, cocktails and shit," Preston said, slurring his words a bit. His teeth were very straight and glaringly white in his handsome tanned face, but a tiny strawberry seed was lodged next to his canine that Crane had no intention of telling him about.

"What do you mean?" Crane asked, bemused.

"You know, you people . . . the gays."

"Oh. Right." Crane stared out over the turquoise water, squinting against the sunlight. What would Preston say if he found out Crane wasn't really gay? "That's just a stereotype."

Crane wished he had Max's flair for mischief. Max would no doubt concoct some bullshit story about the drinking habits of "the gays"—something that made fun of Preston but would go right over his head.

"Yeah, but stereotypes start somewhere, am I right or am I right?" Preston leaned towards Crane. Beneath his expensive cologne, he smelled like old sweat. He levelled a gaze at Crane. "Take the Blacks, for instance. Now, I'm no racist, I've got Black friends, and I've got *all* sorts of respect for them . . . *but*—"

Nothing that started with "I'm not a racist, *but*" went anywhere good. Thankfully, Max plopped down next to Crane, interrupting whatever cringingly awful thing Preston was about to say.

"Did you miss me?" Max asked brightly. He pecked a kiss on Crane's cheek and then nibbled his earlobe.

"Hm," Crane replied, smiling. He pitched his voice so that only Max would hear him. "Let's just say the conversation hasn't exactly been *scintillating*."

"Uh-oh." Max tucked a hand into the wide-open collar of Crane's loose white shirt to rest it on his chest. "That's a shame. I'm having a lovely time. You should see this thing . . . it's *huge*." He smiled at their host. "What do you call this gorgeous yacht of yours?"

"She's called the *Sea La Vie*."

"Seal of E?"

"No, you know, like a pun on the French saying? *C'est la vie*? It means 'This is the life.'"

Crane coughed behind his hand to hide his expression. His French might suck, but even he knew that *c'est la vie* was an expression of resignation or disappointment, as in "oh well . . . what can you do? Such is life."

"Ah. *Clever*," Max said with a chuckle. He shifted his hand so that his index and middle finger trapped Crane's nipple between them in a gentle squeeze.

Crane saw that Preston's eyes followed the motion of Max's hand beneath his shirt—his grin white and toothy, nearly a leer, and Crane decided he really didn't like the way

Preston was looking at Max. It triggered something in his memory about the night they'd all spent together.

"So, where's my wife?" Preston asked, glancing around.

"She had to use the facilities," Max replied, nuzzling closer to Crane.

"Of course. *Women*, am I right?" Preston said, rolling his eyes. He playfully swatted Crane's knee. "Not that you'd know anything about that, huh, fellas?" Laughing, he got to his feet a little unsteadily. "Well, I've got to hit the head myself, and I'll find Vivian and see what's taking Néstor so goddamn long . . ." he said, walking away.

"Oh, god. *Sea La Vie*?" Max said when Preston was out of earshot. He rolled his eyes.

Crane shrugged. "He's rich."

"But, you really should see the size of this thing." Max pinched Crane's nipple harder. "Six big staterooms—those are bedrooms, in yacht-speak—a gym, three hot tubs . . . gawd, the dining room is enormous . . . You sure you don't want to go explore a bit?"

Crane chuckled at the uncharacteristic eagerness in Max's voice. "Aren't you used to this kind of thing? I mean, your stepfather is rich."

"Ouimet's rich and *stingy*. Besides, what makes you think I'd be welcome on his yacht if he had one? I don't know if you realize this, but the man *really* dislikes me." He softly bit the side of Crane's neck. "C'mon . . . let me show you one of the staterooms?"

"I'd be scared to open the closet and find Preston's Nazi memorabilia." Crane winced as Max bit him harder. He laughed. "Or his collection of autographed MAGA hats."

Giggling, Max turned to drape his far leg over Crane's

thigh, half climbing into his lap, facing him. "It's not the *closet* I want to explore."

Crane smiled, running his palm up the back of Max's thigh. He then slid his hand up under the stretchy material of Max's short swim trunks to squeeze his bare ass and said, "And how do you suppose we'd explain our absence to our hosts? Hm?"

Max let out a groan as Crane's fingers skimmed along his lightly furred ass cheek, drifting teasingly close to his pucker. He put his arms around Crane's neck and leaned in to murmur in his ear, "We could just tell them we're just in need of a good fuck. Hell, they'd probably want to join in."

Crane frowned, pulling his hand out of Max's swimsuit. Yeah . . . Preston would probably *love* to get another go at Max, wouldn't he?

"What?" Max cupped Crane's face, staring up at him. "What's wrong?"

"The night we met Preston and Vivian . . . You lied when you said nothing happened."

Max sat up, his dark eyes narrowing as he stared at Crane. "What if I did? Does it really matter?"

"I think it does."

Teeth worrying one side of his bottom lip, Max kept his eyes on Crane's.

"All right," he said at length. "I lied. But maybe I kept things to myself because I know how you can be. I didn't want you to freak out."

"Jesus, I knew it," Crane said, disgusted. "I *knew* it. The way he *looks* at you . . ."

"Looks at *me*?" Max replied, his brows high. He laughed,

shaking his head. "Pump the brakes! *I'm* not the one he put his cock into, *darling*."

"What?" Crane's heart felt like it did a few cartwheels before dropping into the acid pit of his stomach. "What do you mean?"

"Do you want me to spell it out for you?" Max's cheeks dimpled as his grin stretched wide, and he leaned back, tilting his head to scrutinize Crane's expression of disbelief. "You take dick like a champ when you're high as a kite. Can't get enough of it, I swear."

"*Bull*shit." Crane shook his head and pushed Max back onto the padded bench. He wiped his sweating palms on his bright-orange board shorts. "I don't believe you."

"See? You're freaking out." Max sighed. "I don't know what the big deal is, Doc." He reached for Crane's hand, but Crane pulled it out of his grasp.

"I don't believe you," Crane repeated, bile burning the back of his throat.

He was going to be sick. His mind conjured up images of the video of Max in a devil's mask on the ruined bed in the Old Montreal condo. Crane's ass had been inexplicably sore some mornings . . .

However, it was one thing for Max to take advantage of him. It was quite another for some stranger to—

Crane pressed the back of his hand to his mouth and nearly fell getting up. He raced to the side of the yacht, barely making it to the railing before he puked. He gagged and retched a second and third time, tears springing to his eyes.

A cool hand touched his back.

"You okay?" Max asked quietly.

Okay?

No. He wasn't okay. Was there even a word to describe the *horror* he felt? Defiled? Violated?

"Listen, you were having a good time. I swear to god." Max gently rubbed Crane's back.

Crane clung to the metal railing, the foul taste of regurgitated margaritas making his head spin harder. He'd thought tequila was bad going *down* . . .

He groaned.

"No one was forced," Max continued. After a moment, he spoke again, but his voice had taken on a hard edge. "Doc, you know I'd cut the cock off anyone that hurt you."

Crane glanced over at Max.

"*Sure*, you would."

Max shrugged and held out a cocktail napkin to Crane.

Sighing, He accepted the napkin and dabbed his mouth with it. "You'd cut someone's cock off just for the fun of it . . . then blame it on me."

Wide-eyed, Max placed a hand dramatically on his chest. "*Moi?*"

Ignoring him, Crane hung his head over the ship's side again as his stomach roiled.

"Everything okay, buddy?" Preston approached, a whiskey glass in each hand.

Crane turned away, unable to look at the man.

Had Crane been on his knees when Preston penetrated him? Had he been on his back, legs splayed, while the smirking American plowed him?

Oh, god. He gagged, but nothing came out this time.

"I think Rob's had a little too much sun," Max said, rubbing Crane's back again.

"Oh shit, man. Hey, why don't you go inside and have a

little *siesta?*" Preston took a sip from one of the glasses, then gave them another of his bleached smiles. "It'll make you feel better, for sure."

"Thanks."

Max hooked his arm around Crane's waist to help him walk, but Crane pushed him away even though his step was unsteady. He went around the big hot tub, making a beeline towards the patio doors with Max following close behind.

The yacht's interior was ostentatious—a vast dining room with seating for twenty led to a living room with three separate areas to lounge in. Crane looked around, wondering if he should make use of a couch when Max pulled his arm.

"This way."

They went down a flight of stairs and found themselves in a narrow hallway that branched off into bedrooms. Crane chose the first on the right and stood next to the bed, realizing he was too worked up to lie down.

"You okay?" Max asked, touching his shoulder.

Crane jerked away, glaring at him.

"No, I'm not fucking okay. Why would I be fucking okay?" He closed his eyes, trying to calm himself.

"Um. Is this still about the Preston thing?"

With a growl, Crane grabbed Max and flung him down hard on the bed, face-first. When Max landed, his left arm was trapped under his body, so Crane crawled onto the mattress to pin the other against his side with his knee.

"Why would you let him do that to me?" He clenched his teeth, shoving Max's face into the bedding. *"Why?"*

With adrenaline coursing through him, clearing his head, he noticed he was suddenly feeling *much* better.

Max's reply was muffled and unintelligible, but the tone

was glib, so Crane gave him a good smack to the backside. Max let out a yell, but Crane wasn't satisfied. As he held Max down by the back of his neck, he yanked on the young man's swim trunks, exposing his ass, and slapped him again *hard*. This time, Max squealed in pain, trying to wiggle out of Crane's grasp, so he laid down a few more resounding slaps, layering the bright-red handprints until there was a prickle of purple dots at their centre, which he knew would bloom into bruises. Palm stinging, he paused when Max managed to turn his head, screaming for him to stop.

"I lied! I lied! Stop!" Max's face was flushed, and his eyes were red. "I lied!"

"Lied about *what*?" Crane said, raising his hand again. Was that real panic he saw in Max's expression, or was that another lie?

"Preston never fucked you. I lied." With his brow creased in pain, Max swallowed audibly.

"He didn't? You swear?" He tilted his head, ready to swat Max again.

"I swear! Don't hit me again. *Please?*"

Crane lowered his hand, breathing heavily, but didn't release Max.

"*Why* do you get so much pleasure out of torturing me?" Crane asked wearily.

A cheeky grin instantly replaced Max's pained look, and Crane knew he would probably never get the real truth out of him. His ass was Schrödinger's ass—simultaneously fucked and unfucked. Crane sighed.

"Okay, what *did* happen that night?"

Max let out a little giggle. "Wouldn't you like to know."

"Did he fuck *you*?" Crane asked, his temper rising again.

He exhaled hard, trying to shoo away the image of Preston bending Max over and spitting on his hole. Preston probably had a big dick too.

Chuckling again, Max shrugged, a glint of mischief in his eye.

"Did he?" He frowned, his chest getting tight as he breathed through clenched teeth. "Wait . . . did you fuck *her*?"

"What if I said . . . yes?"

"To which?"

"Now *that's* interesting," Max said, his dimples appearing again. "Which would make you angrier, I wonder?"

Furious, Crane tightened his hold on Max's neck, wanting to rip his head right off his shoulders, but then he noticed what was on the wooden headboard. He let go of Max and reached for the finial—sure enough, it unscrewed in his hand.

"What are you doing?" Max asked, lifting his head off the mattress. When he saw what Crane was holding, his eyes went very round. "No."

The polished wood finial was shaped like a teardrop resting on a flared base. Crane felt his face stretch into a maniacal grin. The widest part of the finial was nearly the size of an apple.

"Oh, *yes*."

"Don't you dare," Max said, crawling forward on the bed to escape Crane.

Crane grabbed a handful of his swim trunks, but Max slid out of them and toppled to the floor next to the bed. Crane was on him in an instant, flattening him under his weight. He lost hold of the finial for a moment in the struggle, but after a futile attempt to wriggle free, Max was subdued facedown once again, Crane sitting astride his lower back. He picked up the finial, spat on it, then pried open Max's ass cheeks to find his hole.

"*Please.* Really. Nothing happened. Nothing at all. You were going on and on about ten sorts of nonsense . . . oh my god, Dennis, *don't—*"

The top of the finial slid in without a hitch. Crane chuckled, leaning forward to add spit to Max's pucker.

"I'm saying *no*, Dennis. *No.*"

The panic sounded real in Max's voice as Crane started pushing the finial further into him.

"Please? Oh, *fuck.*"

Max gasped and then panted rapidly as his asshole began to open wide, the bed knob stretching him out in tiny increments. "I swear. I swear to god you were just talking crazy, and we were watching you, and no one fucked anyone . . . there was no fucking at all! *Ow. Ow, fuck.* Shit. You took your pants off because you thought your dick was a snake for some reason, and—*oh my god,* you're going to tear my ass."

"Stop wiggling, you little shit," Crane said, applying more pressure after he spat again. "It's barely in."

"Jesus Christ, Doc. You can't do this. *Please.* You're hurting me. Doc, please—" Max stopped struggling, and Crane felt him tense. "Wait, what was that?"

Crane cocked his head, pausing in his attempt to impale Max with the wooden bed knob. He'd heard something too: a rustle and a thump. He stood, releasing Max and approached the closet. There it was again—quiet movement behind the sliding door. He glanced at Max, who pulled the finial out of his ass, tossing it onto the bed before joining him.

"What do you think it is?" Max whispered.

"Open the door and find out," Crane whispered back. He'd joked about Nazi memorabilia, but what if Preston collected something else? Like . . . underaged sex slaves that he kept tied up in closets? He snorted. It was probably just something that had shifted because of their horseplay.

"Hello?" Max said, stepping forward. He put a hand on the door and looked over his shoulder at Crane before pushing it open.

An overweight, middle-aged woman in a white-and-blue maid's outfit spilled out of the closet, falling against Crane.

"Are you all right?" he asked, helping the woman to stand. "What on earth were you doing in there?"

The woman straightened her white maid's cap over her thick salt-and-pepper hair, staring wide-eyed at Crane before glancing at Max. Max grinned and put his hands over his crotch to hide his dick.

"I . . . I hear you come," the woman said in a thick accent. "I hide closet. Please . . . don't say?"

"Don't tell who? Preston?" asked Max, his brows high.

"Yes. Master Preston. He say we stay"—she made shooing motion with both hands—"hiding when are guests."

Crane scowled. "He makes you stay hidden when there are guests aboard?"

"Yes. No looks good for guests," the woman answered, looking frightened. She pulled away from him. "*Por favor?* I go."

At Crane's nod, the woman peered out the door, checking both ways before she made her escape.

"Remind me again why we're on this asshole's boat?" Crane asked.

"Seemed like a good idea at the time," Max replied,

pulling up his green swim trunks. "So, are you going to lie down and rest?"

Crane thought about it for a second, then shook his head. His nausea was gone, and he felt fine, apart from a faint headache.

"Okay. I'll meet you topside." Max picked up the wooden finial.

"Why? Where are you going with that?"

"I'm going to go put it in my bag. I figure you can try again later with some real lube."

Crane squinted against the sun as he walked back out onto the deck, where Preston was speaking to a tall dark-skinned man in a crew uniform. From Preston's body language, Crane could tell he was angry about something, but he only caught the last word before the crewman was sent away: *her.*

Brow furrowed, he joined his host beneath the sunshade.

"Hey Rob-o, my man," Preston said, his smile bright. He put a hand on Crane's shoulder close to his neck and squeezed it—a textbook display of male dominance. "Feeling better?"

It annoyed Crane to no end that he and Preston were the same height—he would have enjoyed looking down on the intolerable American. "Yeah."

"You look better." Preston released Crane's shoulder to give him a light tap on the cheek, then motioned for him to sit down. "Did you manage to nap? You weren't gone very long."

"Nah—turns out I didn't need it." Crane sat down at the opposite end of the big U-shaped couch, still closer to Preston than he liked, and forced a smile. It was an effort to hide the revulsion he felt for the man. "Is everything all right?"

"What do you mean? Oh, that just now?" He motioned in the direction the crewman had gone. "Well, Viv's being a little antisocial, that's all. Don't worry; she'll join us in a bit." Preston rested one tanned arm along the seatback, crossing his leg so his ankle rested on the opposite knee. "Speaking of better halves . . . where's yours?"

Stealing pieces of your ship to stick up his ass. "I think he went to go get a glass of water."

"That's what my crew is here for," Preston replied with a laugh. Then, to demonstrate, he motioned to the crewmate that hovered nearby, beckoning him to approach. "Still want that whiskey? I have a Japanese one I haven't had a chance to try yet. Oh, and it looks like we have a good Dalmore aboard today."

"Sure," Crane said. "Whichever."

Preston turned back to the crewmate to ask for the whiskeys just as Max and Vivian emerged from the yacht's interior.

Right away, Crane noticed something was amiss. Vivian had put on huge Jackie Onassis sunglasses and a big floppy hat, but even with her face partially obscured, he could tell she had been crying—her nose was red and cheeks blotchy. Then he saw the fresh bruises around her wrist. Vivian saw him looking at her and crossed her arms over her chest, hiding her injury. She gave Crane a tight smile before sitting down next to him. Max stood for a moment, his eyes on Vivian, then sat down in the gulf between her and her husband.

"There you are, honey," Preston said cheerily. "Do you have something to say to our guests?"

"I'm sorry I was being so rude," Vivian said quietly, not looking at either of them.

"Not at all," Crane replied, anger like a hot ball of lead in his gut. His opinion of the man had sunk to the lowest of depths.

However, he discovered it could sink even lower a few moments later.

"Now . . . how about we have ourselves a little fun while we head back to port?" Preston said, accepting the glass of whiskey handed to him.

Crane took his own glass but just held it, not liking the coy edge to Preston's tone. He frowned.

"What do you mean?"

Preston smirked and began toying with the button on his khaki shorts.

"I was thinking Dan here could give me another little blowie?" He said, using Max's assumed name. "The one he gave me the other night's been on my mind allll day."

Jaw clenched, Crane turned to Max, and Max winked at him before sliding off the seat to position himself between Preston's knees. *Lying about lying about lying about lying . . .*

Eyes locked on Crane, Preston took a sip of whiskey and gave him a gloating smile as he gently stroked Max's dark curls back. "This is the Dalmore. Let me know what you think."

Crane jerkily lifted his glass to his lips and took a sip, but his throat was so thick with anger that he couldn't swallow. He sat there with whiskey burning in his mouth as Max pulled Preston's cock out of his pants. He'd been right—Preston was well endowed.

Once he could swallow without choking, he downed the

whiskey quickly and held out his glass to the crewmate who stood by. "Another."

"Oh, Viv, you gotta come here and watch this. Danny boy here gives better head than you ever have. Come, maybe you'll learn something," Preston said, putting his head back on the seat, his eyes closing as he let out a deep groan.

"Okay," Vivian said, getting to her feet. She glanced at Crane, her expression unreadable, and went to stand next to her husband while Max sucked on his fat cock.

The second glass of whiskey went down quicker than the first.

"Another."

The taxi pulled away from the marina in Cancun and headed south along the highway toward Playa del Carmen. The sun was low in the sky, trimming the fluffy clouds in gold and pink above lush vegetation. Stands of palm trees occasionally blotted out the view of the sky, giving Crane only glimpses of the gilded clouds through fluttering leaves, like burlesque dancers teasing with their feather fans. It was beautiful, but Crane was tired and angry and unpleasantly tipsy.

"I'm starving," Max said, then yawned. "Tired too. Why does the sun and fresh air make me *so* tired?" He turned towards Crane, a sleepy grin on his face, and leaned in for a kiss. Crane recoiled, pushing him back, and met the taxi driver's eyes in the rearview. The man shook his head, muttering a slur in Spanish just loud enough for Crane to hear him.

"Stop that," Crane snapped, shoving Max again.

"Who cares?" Max replied, his tone flippant. "It's not like he's going to kick us out. Not if he wants the other half *de su tarifa*," he said, raising his voice.

The taxi driver huffed out a breath, shaking his head.

"It's not that." Crane looked out the window again. "I know where your mouth's been."

"Well . . . nerts to you."

They sat in silence as the taxi raced through one tiny town after another, past a golf course and a strip mall. Finally, Crane sighed angrily, unable to contain himself any longer.

"I can't believe you *did* that. And right in front of me."

"What was I supposed to do? For all I know, he would have sent us overboard in a dinghy if I said no to sucking him off. And I don't know about you, but rowing for hours and hours on end is *not* my idea of a good time."

Rubbing his forehead, Crane glanced over.

"*Nothing happened the other night. I swear to gawwwd,*" Crane said, pitching his voice higher.

"Is that supposed to be me?" Max laughed. "Listen, Doc; I don't know why you're so surprised."

"Honestly, I don't either," Crane replied, looking away. Then, after another long silence, he spoke up again. "He beats her."

"Yeah. I know."

"And you're okay with that?"

"No."

There was something so menacing in that single syllable that Crane tensed involuntarily, but when he met Max's gaze, there was nothing but amusement in his dark eyes.

"*You* beat me," Max said.

"I do *not*," Crane replied, going back to watching the palms zip by.

"My ass is sore."

"It's not the same, and you know it."

Max chuckled, and this time when he reached out his hand to Crane, Crane took it. They rode the rest of the way in silence.

Finally, the cab pulled up to the condo, but instead of following Max inside, Crane decided to pick up something for supper.

"I'll be back in a bit. Do you want extra chimichurri on your *choripán*?

Crane stood in the tiny Argentinian restaurant down the street, waiting for his order, when he saw his own face on the small television bolted up in the corner of the room. Unable to breathe, he watched the Spanish-language news feature the oft-broadcasted video of him being led down the courthouse steps last November, followed by a schematic of the prison where he'd been incarcerated for six long months. They went on for a while, maybe discussing theories about how he'd managed to escape, then suddenly, there was a bright-yellow map of Mexico on the screen with both Cancún and Playa del Carmen shaded in red.

"Oh god," he whispered as his face again took centre stage on the small screen.

Nervously, he looked around, pulling his straw hat down further.

Thankfully, they had chosen the picture from his Québec driver's license and not his mug shot. The photo on the television was taken about six months before he'd even met Max. The man up on the dusty screen was clean-cut. Respectable. His eyes were clear. He had a nice haircut. *That* man had a loving wife, and a comfortable home, and he was just weeks away from completing his doctoral degree . . . *so* full of hope for the future. Crane snorted.

No, the man on the news was nothing like the wild-eyed, scruffy, wretched creature Crane had become. No one would recognize him. But, somehow, the authorities had discovered he was in Mexico, and that was really fucking bad.

He had to get back to Max.

Time to get out of Dodge, eh, Doc?

Heart pounding, Crane scanned the restaurant again and noticed a heavyset man wearing a too-small fedora standing by the doorway. He had a distinct impression that the man had just looked away.

Shit. Was he watching me?

Crane frowned, wondering why the man seemed so familiar. He seen that tiny fedora before.

The man glanced his way, and Crane quickly turned back to the television, where they were now showing a black-and-white video. The grainy image was of a man tied to a chair. He looked like he was screaming, his mouth open in a perfect black circle as he tossed his head from side to side.

What the hell?

He squinted, wishing the glare from the neon sign wasn't

obscuring part of the image because there was something behind the seated man that he *knew* he'd seen somewhere . . .

"Señor?"

After murmuring a quiet *gracias* to the man who handed over his order, Crane practically sprinted the four blocks to the condo and was confused when he found the door locked. He knocked twice, listened, and when Max didn't answer, he dug around in his pocket for the key, hoping he had it with him.

"There you are," he muttered, jamming it into the lock, but he froze when he opened the door. Standing in the tiny kitchen with her back to him was a woman. "Hello?" he said, hoping it was just Max in a wig and dress, but when she turned, he nearly dropped the bag on the floor.

Mouth dry, he blinked at the woman. "Mrs. Ouimet?"

Évangéline gaped up at him. He'd forgotten that she had the same dark eyes as her son.

"*You* . . ." she said in a harsh whisper, backing up against the kitchen island. "What are *you* doing here?"

"I'd ask the same of you." Crane took a wary step into the room to place the paper bag on the table. "What are you doing here? How did you get in?"

"Where is Édouard? Where is my son?" she asked, ignoring his questions. Her thin lips had pulled tight over her teeth as she hissed the words at him.

Crane took a half step back—he saw nothing but pure malice now that she was over the shock of seeing him.

"Where is he, you *monster*?" Évangéline continued, her voice harsh with rage. "You fucking pervert."

She switched to rapid-fire French; the only words he recognized were *prison* and *tabarnak*.

Her eyes were filled with rage as she railed at him. "How could you hurt my baby? *How?*"

Crane's jaw tightened at her words.

"*Me* hurt your *baby?*" He gave a humourless laugh. "*Me* hurt *him? He* fucked up *my* life. *He* hurt *me.* Don't you see that *he's* the monster? How fucking blind do you have to be to miss the fact that your son is a goddamn psychopath?"

Glaring at him, Évangéline shook her head. "No. You're th—"

"Actually, *you're* the one who made him what he is, *aren't* you? That's right. You and his father. Where were *you* when *he* was abusing your *baby?* Hm? Where were you when his father was molesting him? Where the *fuck* were you? What kind of a fucking mother are you?" Crane said, his voice rising to a shout.

With a shriek, she launched herself at him, and he shoved her back, recoiling from the sharp red nails that raked at his face. He darted into the kitchen, keeping the centre island between them, and cursed when she managed to grab the big serrated knife from the cutting board before he could stop her.

"I'm going to *kill* you." Breathing hard, she held the knife with both hands, brandishing it at him. "But first, I'm going to cut your pervert cock off."

Crane ducked to the side as she jabbed the knife toward him but misstepped and crashed into the cupboards. His stumble gave Évangéline time to reach him, and he desperately swung a fist at her, hoping to force her back before she managed to stab him. Instead of retreating, she ducked under his arm and brought the knife up, but this time, he was ready and slammed his palm into the side of her elbow, sending the blade spinning through the air to land with a clatter on the tile. Heart pounding, he grabbed her wrists as she lunged at him again and managed to turn her around, sending her flying with a hard shove.

Évangéline gave a short grunt as her head struck the side of the kitchen island, and she dropped like a rag doll, her neck at an odd angle.

"Oh my god," Crane said, falling to his knees. He crawled towards her. "Mrs. Ouimet? Évangéline?"

The woman had a deep gash on her forehead, and blood ran from it as if from a faucet.

Gurgling quietly, she blinked up at him through the blood. Crane could see her pupils were different sizes. Suddenly she gasped, her jaw jerking from side to side a few times, and went still with a rattling sigh.

Crane's stomach clenched, and he turned away, afraid he would be sick. Panic choked his lungs. He gasped air like a fish out of water, black spots swarming his vision. There wasn't even room for thought in his mind, not yet—there was only a high-pitched whine echoing in his head, obscuring everything else.

Then he shuddered, took a deep breath, and pressed his hands to his mouth to stifle his cries, his palms tacky with Évangéline's blood.

Oh my god, what did I do? What did I do? He crawled backwards out of the puddle of blood, his eyes fixed on the dead woman's blank stare, then he turned and struggled to his feet, running almost blind down the hallway to the bathroom, where he slammed the door behind him.

He'd just killed someone. Someone *died*, and it was *his* fault. Tears obscured his vision. When he wiped at his eyes, Évangéline's blood smeared across his face. Horrified, he climbed into the bathtub and wrapped his arms around his knees.

What am I going to do? He felt like screaming or throwing up or both. *Max will know what to do. Max will know.*

Crane rocked slowly in place, trying to calm his racing mind. Max *would* know what to do . . . but it was his fucking *mother*. What would he do when he found his mother dead on the kitchen floor?

Oh my god.

Crane pulled his bloody T-shirt up to hide his face and block everything out.

I killed his fucking mother. He's going to kill me. What am I going to do? What am I going to do? What am I going to do?

"What are you *doing?*"

Startled, Crane stopped rocking, sitting paralyzed with his hands like claws over the top of his head, the bottom of the T-shirt clenched between his teeth.

"Doc?"

Crane's heart was beating so fast he was gasping for breath again as he slowly lowered his hands, pulling down the shirt to uncover just his eyes. Max was staring down at him, his forehead deeply wrinkled.

"I . . . I'm sorry," Crane managed, the low rasp of his voice muffled by the fabric.

Max's dark brows slowly rose, and he tilted his head, looking mildly amused.

"I was just wondering if you were coming back to bed." Max scrubbed a hand through his messy curls and yawned. "But I guess I'll leave you to . . . whatever"—he gestured at Crane in the bathtub—"this is."

"Back . . . to bed?" Crane whispered.

"Yeah, *bed*. You know the big squishy rectangle where we lie unconscious for hours at a time? That is, when you're not getting a bit of the old in-out."

Confused, Crane stared up at him. Max had gone to bed? It seemed impossible that he'd slept through all the screaming —*could* he have?

"Your mother . . ." Crane said nervously, shaking his head. The T-shirt fell around his shoulders, uncovering the rest of his face, and he rubbed his numb lips with the back of his hand before continuing. "It was an accident, you have to believe me."

"What *about* my mother?" Max's expression sobered.

"She was here when I got back." Crane looked in the direction of the kitchen, his throat so raw he had a hard time swallowing. "We argued in the kitchen, and she attacked me."

"Ah. Hm. My *mother*." Max nodded thoughtfully for a moment, but then the corners of his eyes crinkled as an indulgent smile dimpled his cheeks. "My mother attacked you in the kitchen. Ah ha. Gotcha."

"I'm serious. And . . . what happened after was an accident."

Max chuckled. "What? Did you *accidentally* put your dick into her? Gosh, is that what you're trying to say? Are you going to be my new daddy?"

"Max . . . *stop*. Listen to me. She's dead."

"Wow, that's morbid. So, you had a bad dream about killing my mom through rumpy pumpy? Weird but okay. And you came in here to . . . what? Hide from me?"

Crane's fear began to dissolve under Max's teasing. He frowned and awkwardly rose to his feet.

"It wasn't a fucking dream," he said, stepping out of the

bathtub. "She's lying out there. Just go and fucking see for yourself." As he spoke, the edge of hysteria crept back into his voice, so he wrapped his arms around himself to keep from trembling.

Max looked at him strangely, then lifted his hands in a placating gesture.

"All right, all right. If it means so much to you, I'll go look."

Clenching his jaw, Crane watched Max leave the bathroom. The silence was deafening and then Max cried out.

"Oh my god. Mom? Are you okay? What happened?"

Stunned, Crane ran to the kitchen to find Max cradling his arms around empty space.

As soon as Max saw him, he started giggling. "What's that, Mom? *Jesus wept* . . . are you saying Doc's dick is a deadly weapon?"

Crane cast around in a daze, searching for any sign of the struggle that had happened only moments earlier, but there was nothing there. No body. No blood. Breath hitching in his chest, he looked down at his hands and saw they were spotless too, as was his T-shirt.

"I don't understand."

Max dropped the pantomime and grinned crookedly at Crane.

"I told you. Just a dream, Doc. Now, come back to bed."

"It *can't* have been a dream. How could it be? I never even went to bed." He breathed deeply a few times to calm his nerves, his eyes on the clean tiles where he'd left the woman's body. "No, she was definitely here. I swear to god. I came back from the Argentinian place, and she was just . . . standing right there and—"

"Hold up," Max said, frowning. "We had *choripán* two days ago."

"What? No . . . I *just* went out for it . . ." Crane licked his lips, shaking his head. He felt light-headed, so he leaned against the kitchen island. He scowled. "Stop it. Don't play games. Not now."

"Doc . . . what day do you think it is?" Max asked quietly after staring at him in silence for a few moments.

Crane's heartbeat kicked up another notch. He blinked at Max, nervously wiping his palms on his shorts. More than anything, it was the genuine-looking concern on Max's face that was scaring him.

"It's the nineteenth," Crane replied. "Sunday. We just came back from the cruise with . . ."

At Max's slow headshake, he trailed off.

"It's the *twenty-first*, Doc," Max said, a deep crease between his brows.

"Stop it," Crane repeated in a hoarse voice. He could barely hear himself above the cymbal crash of his heartbeat. "Look. The food is still there . . ."

He walked unsteadily over to the paper bag he'd dropped on the table and opened it to show Max. When Max shook his head again, Crane looked down into the bag and gaped in confusion. The only thing inside were stacks of American hundred-dollar bills. "What the . . . It can't—" His body gave an involuntary shiver. "I don't . . . I don't understand what's going on."

"That's some money I brought home earlier today, Doc. I have to deliver it tomorrow. But, never mind about that." He came closer and peered up at Crane. "What's the *last* thing you remember?"

"I just told you. We came home in a taxi, and I left you here and went to go get supper."

Max nodded. "You did. And you came home, and we ate it."

Crane shook his head frantically. "No. That can't—" He twisted his hands together, concentrating. "Oh *god*," he said, remembering what had happened at the restaurant. "Max, the police know we're in Mexico—"

"Yes. You *told* me. *Two days* ago." The muscles rolled in Max's jaw as he stared at Crane with uncharacteristic gravity. "And you said you saw a man acting suspicious. You thought you'd seen him before—a big man in a small hat. And I told you not to worry about it. You're just being paranoid. We're totally safe."

In a daze, Crane took a step back. There was no way that Max could know about the news and the man . . . *unless* he was speaking the truth about it being Tuesday. Crane swallowed thickly—he was close to tears.

"What's happening to me?" He dropped into the kitchen chair, all feeling gone in his legs. Was it drugs? The last time Max had dosed him, he'd also lost two days, but this felt completely different. "Did you give me that . . . *víbora* drug again?"

"No. I swear."

"What if it's an after-effect?"

"No. No, I think there's something else going on here." Max surprised Crane by reaching out to touch his forehead with the back of his hand. "Jesus, you're burning up."

Without another word, he left Crane in the kitchen and returned a minute later, dressed. "Come."

"Where are we going?"

"*We're* not going anywhere. I just want you to lie down while I'm gone." He led Crane to the couch. "And *stay put.*"

"Where are you going?" Crane said, lying down with Max's assistance. He shivered again, weak as a kitten. His head felt weird.

"I'm going to get help."

SEVEN
THE PROBLEM WITH CRANE'S BRAIN

WEDNESDAY, NOVEMBER 22ND

Dr. Aguilar shone a flashlight in Crane's eyes, flicking it from one to the other a few times, then he sat back with a pensive look.

"You say he caught a stomach virus?" the man asked Max, his black brows high in his handsome face. He spoke English with only the barest hint of an accent. "Maybe a norovirus?"

Max nodded. "Yeah. A few weeks back."

"Was it severe?" the doctor asked.

"It wasn't *not* severe," Max replied with a shrug.

"I spent almost four days in the bathroom," Crane clarified. "I can't remember the last time I was so sick. It was awful. And it took a full week for my stomach to settle completely."

"Hm." The man rubbed his forehead tiredly, staring off into the distance. It was almost four o'clock in the morning. "It *could* be you have a little swelling of the brain."

Crane sat up in alarm. "That's serious."

The doctor tilted his head from side to side, his lips pressed together. Then, at length, he answered, "Might not be. Have you had bad headaches? Stiff neck? Troubles walking? No?" He frowned. "Okay, did you have a severe illness as a child?" After Crane had shaken his head again, the man sighed. "Well, encephalitis following a bout of norovirus is not *that* rare, I suppose. Most of the time, it's not even noticeable, and it just goes away on its own. What concerns me is this loss of time and these vivid hallucinations . . . but, then again, you're not exhibiting the more worrying symptoms." Dr. Aguilar scratched at the collar of his blue-striped pyjamas. "We could do a little test. It's not conclusive, but it could tell us if there is evidence of swelling and perhaps in which part of the brain."

"Yes. Can we do that? Is it painful?" Crane asked.

Dr. Aguilar chuckled. "No. Just a sheet of paper and a drawing implement, *por favor.*"

Max ripped a sheet out of the notepad by the door, and the doctor placed it in front of Crane, handing him a pen from his bag when Max came up short.

"Now. Draw a clock and make the hands point to, uh . . . three o'clock."

Crane nodded and dutifully drew a circle and placed the numbers around the inside, drawing a short hand pointing to the three and a longer one pointing to the twelve.

Whistling, Max shook his head. "Wow," he said, picking up the page. "It's just like on Hannibal."

"What?" Crane took the page back from him.

On the show, Will Graham had drawn numbers that skewed to one side, but there was nothing wrong with Crane's clock at all. At least that he could see.

"It seems the inflammation is there, but is not localized on a particular side." Dr. Aguilar reached over the paper to point to the clock. "It is disordered, but not severely so."

"I don't see it," Crane replied, worry making his voice a touch hoarse. "What . . . what should we do?"

"Well, you could get a blood test at the tourist clinic, but I fear we won't know for certain what's going on until you get an MRI, and the closest place you can do that is in Cancún."

"Is that what you think we should do?" asked Max. He was sitting very still on the couch next to Crane, his hands clutched together between his knees, the absolute picture of a concerned loved one.

"You want my honest opinion?" Dr. Aguilar asked.

"Yes, please," Crane replied.

"Give it a few days. Stay in bed. Read some books. Drink plenty of liquids. If your symptoms get worse, *then* you go to the private hospital in Cancún. No need to worry yourself . . . not yet."

"Really?" Crane asked, skeptical.

"Mr. Cooper here can keep a close eye on you . . . check your temperature, etcetera. And you can always send for me again. I'm only down the street." The doctor yawned. "Oh"— he fished around in his leather satchel and pulled out a few small packets—"take these. They're for fever and inflammation . . . mostly. One in the morning. One at night. Always with food. Maybe they'll help," he said, dropping them into Crane's palm. "Goodnight. Good luck, Mr. Montagnet."

Crane watched Max escort the doctor to the door, his brow deeply furrowed. Then, when Max came back to the couch, Crane scoffed.

"Good luck? *Maybe* they'll help? Where the hell did you find this guy?" He peered at the packets in his hand, but the writing was all in Spanish.

"Dr. Aguilar's a good guy and a great doctor. He knows what he's talking about." Max frowned. "We're lucky he lives so close."

"Oh." Crane frowned, wondering how Max knew the man. "Okay. Sorry . . . It's late, and I'm tired and cranky, and supposedly, my brain is swelling."

Max smirked, nodding. Then he held out his hands. "Come on, Doc. Upsy-daisy. Let's get you back to bed."

Sighing, Crane reached up and let Max help him to his feet. He swayed, dismayed by how shaky he was after his ordeal. It was a good thing Max was there to help him. He'd probably be crawling on all fours otherwise.

Max fussed about, making sure he was comfortable, then he went to get him a glass of water to swallow the pill down with. Afterwards, he curled up next to Crane, holding his hand. Even though Crane knew it was just Max playing pretend . . . the gesture did make him feel better.

"So, what in tarnation would you and my mother argue about that would make her pull a knife on you?" Max asked after a while. "Was it because you kidnapped me and did *suuuper* improper things to me?" His grin went impish, evidently *trying* to spoil their quiet moment.

Annoyed, Crane scowled and looked over at Max. "No. Actually, it was about your father and what *he* did to you. Not your stepfather. I mean Maurice Richard."

Max's eyes got comically wide. "The . . . hockey player? *Rocket* Richard?"

Crane stared at him, unblinking. "Wait . . . you said that

was your father's name. I even looked him up. You said he was in jail for molesting you."

"I said *what* now? When?"

"Uh . . . a week ago?" Crane squinted at the ceiling, thinking. "Maybe a week and a half?"

"Well, my father's name was Michel Pelletier, not Maurice Richard. He was a truck driver from Rivière-du-Loup." Max lifted himself up to look down at Crane, bracing himself on his elbow. "And he didn't molest me. At least . . . I don't think he did—he died when I was three. A car accident. I don't remember him, really. I get flashes sometimes, like, when I smell the cheap cologne he used to wear. But I don't *think* he was a kiddie fiddler."

"So . . . that conversation never happened?" Crane's mind was reeling again. "I hallucinated it?"

"Seems like it. What else did I say?"

Crane started from the beginning, telling Max everything he remembered, then he frowned.

"Are Tor and VPN a real thing?"

Max chuckled. "Yes."

"If I hallucinated the whole conversation, why would I know about those? I've never heard of either."

"Yes, you have, Doc. We use VPN all the time to watch American Netflix." Max narrowed his eyes and touched Crane's forehead again. "Oh, good. I think your fever's already going down."

"Well . . . what about Tor?"

"Tor is a darknet. I use it for contracts because it's super private and almost untraceable. That's how I move our money around too. You've seen me use the Tor browser. Remember?

You asked why it's got an onion for a logo, and I explained about layers of privacy."

"Oh. Yeah. I think I remember that," Crane fibbed, feeling sheepish. He often regretted asking Max to explain anything technical because after five minutes, everything started to sound like gibberish, and his eyes would glaze over as he inevitably tuned him out. "So, I imagined the whole thing."

"Sure did."

"It all seemed so real." He thought about the last few days. "When we were on the yacht, did we end up in a bedroom?"

"It's called a *stateroom* on a yacht, but yup."

"And I tried to um . . ." Red-faced, Crane grimaced, thinking about the bed knob, and gestured vaguely.

Max giggled. "Yup."

"And there was a maid hiding in the closet?"

"Yup."

"And when we went back out, you gave Preston a blowjob?"

"What? *Ew*, no," Max said with a laugh.

Crane narrowed his eyes at him. It seemed a little too convenient that the only thing he'd imagined on their cruise was Max servicing Preston.

"What? I swear," Max said, leaning down to peck a kiss on his lips.

"And you were never molested by your father?"

"Only by you, darling."

"And I didn't kill your mother."

"Nope." Max tilted his head, and a comma appeared between his brows, his eyes a little distant. "Huh . . . it makes sense now."

"What does?"

"You said you saw yourself on the news—that the cops knew where you were . . ."

"Did I imagine that too?"

"Think about it, darling. I made you promise to stay away from the news not too long before that, right? Doesn't it sound like your poor swollen brain cooked up something tasty for your paranoia?"

Crane remembered the strange grainy black-and-white video of the man screaming. It definitely seemed like a nightmare vision in hindsight. "Yeah. I think you're right."

Max nodded and squeezed his thigh gently. His dark eyes crinkled with his smile. "You just need some rest, and I'm *sure* you'll be fine. You'll see."

Sighing, Crane pressed the heels of his hands against his eyes. It was amazing how frighteningly real everything had seemed—he really hoped the doctor was right about the swelling going down on its own with a bit of rest.

"But . . . it feels like all I've been doing is resting for the last two weeks. How is more rest going to help?"

"Yeaahh, well, first you were recovering from your stomach issues. And then you were recovering from *la víbora* . . . heh, uh, twice." Max frowned and tapped his finger against his lips. "I guess I *probably* made things worse, didn't I?"

"Probably. You shouldn't drug people," Crane replied, allowing himself a small smile.

"So you've mentioned." Max rolled his eyes. "Okay, I'm sorry."

"Bullshit."

"I'm serious." Max tilted his head as he chewed the side of his lip. "I feel bad that I didn't notice you were sick."

"I'm pretty sure you're incapable of feeling bad . . . but I guess I'll give you points for trying. The little catch in your voice is a nice touch."

Max's smile flashed wide for a second, then he sobered, the look of concern back. "Is there anything I can get for you, Doc?"

"Actually, yes—I want to see your laptop," Crane said. "Can you get it?"

Max quirked his eyebrows at Crane, but he got out of bed without a word and returned with the MacBook. "Here," he said, handing it over.

Crane shimmied himself up to a half-sitting position and opened the laptop. Instead of Max's desktop, he was presented with the login screen. He turned the computer towards Max, watching him with a bemused expression.

"Log in as you."

Max leaned forward and entered his password, and Crane stared at the chaotic desktop. It looked the same as it had the other day, down to the folder labelled "randos – tentacles, scales, and dogdicks," but there was one exception—the Mary folder was missing.

"Did you take videos of Mary?" Crane asked.

"Mary?" Max said, yawning as he curled up against his side again.

"My wife?"

"Silly . . . why would I take videos of your wife?"

Crane scanned Max's desktop again in case he had missed the folder. It was possible—his glasses were in the other room. Then he shook his head, exasperated. It just wasn't there.

He turned to Max to ask him what *he* remembered of that day, if anything, but Max had already fallen asleep. Brow furrowed, Crane clicked on the little fox browser icon and pulled up Wikipedia, where he did a search for Maurice Richard. The list was the same as before, minus the convicted rapist entry.

Something genuinely felt . . . *off* about his memories. Crane looked over at Max and narrowed his eyes.

EIGHT
THE BOY IN THE BIKINI

TUESDAY, NOVEMBER 28TH

Crane felt better than he had in a long time. It had taken a week of bed rest and more of Dr. Aguilar's medicine, but his head was now clear, and his energy was back. His mood had also vastly improved, a large part of that because Max had played the perfect nursemaid the entire time. He'd gone to the English language bookstore on La Quinta to get some books for Crane, had cooked all sorts of comfort food, and spent hours just hanging out with him in bed, watching movies. Max had been so attentive and thoughtful that Crane's niggling doubts about some of his hallucinations had nearly faded.

The previous evening, Dr. Aguilar had passed by to check on him and had given him a clean bill of health, which was *great* news because Crane was thoroughly sick of lying around in bed all day. Yawning, he sat up.

"Max?" he called out, but the condo was silent. He found a pair of clean board shorts in a drawer and was surprised when he saw they stayed up without the drawstring tied. Brows high, he studied himself in the warped mirror above the dresser. It seemed like bed rest and plenty of good food had fleshed him out a little. Certainly, it was the heaviest he'd been in over a year, and with the bags under his eyes gone, he was less haggard. Rubbing his lightly stubbled cheek—Max had shaved him the day before—he turned to check out his profile and smiled.

Looking good. Feeling good.

Now if he could only do away with the looming dread of being discovered by the authorities . . .

"Max?" he tried again, raking his hair back to tidy it. Where was he?

When the living room and kitchen turned up empty, Crane assumed Max had gone out, but there was no note on the counter or message on his phone.

There was a piece of paper on the coffee table, but when he turned it over, he saw it was just the clock that Dr. Aguilar had made him draw the first night he'd come over. At the time, the clock had looked completely normal to him, but ever since his brain had recovered, he could see what he'd actually drawn. It was more of a flattened oval than a circle, and instead of the numbers going around the inside, they were in a jumbled heap at the top—the hands weren't even inside the clock, and they both pointed in the same direction.

Shaking his head, Crane laughed uneasily. He felt lucky to be alive, even though the doctor hadn't seemed worried at all. Crane peered closer at the paper. His brain had definitely been going haywire—the number four he'd drawn wasn't even the way he usually wrote them.

Crane crumpled the paper and tossed it in the garbage,

and then noticed the patio door was slightly ajar. Pushing it open, he grinned and stepped out onto the balcony.

"There you a—" He stopped in his tracks. Crane stared bug-eyed at Max who was reading, reclined on a towel draped over the old plastic lounger. "What are you *wearing*?" he managed in a hoarse whisper.

Max set aside his book and smiled as he looked up at Crane demurely through his dark lashes.

"Do you like it?" he asked in a soft purr, languidly rising to his feet to show off his outfit when Crane still couldn't get his voice to work.

Two minuscule triangles of bubble-gum pink cloth *barely* covered Max's nipples, and below, a third small triangle of pink bulged lewdly with anatomy it wasn't designed to hold. Then, as Crane continued to stare in stunned silence, Max pulled aside the top of the world's tiniest bikini to uncover a well-defined triangle of pale skin around his small rosy-brown nipple—he'd obviously been out in the sun for a while—and Crane was suddenly overwhelmed with a strange desire to rub his cock over those crisp tan lines.

Max's gaze dropped, and he chuckled. "I guess you do like it, eh, Doc?" he murmured.

Heart pounding, Crane glanced down at the growing tent in his shorts and cleared his throat.

"It's, uh . . . *yeah*," he replied quietly, focusing on the bikini bottom again. The smooth, naked base of Max's cock was clearly visible an inch above the satiny fabric. And there was *something* about the sight of it. Something was . . .. *different*. He frowned.

Smooth . . . naked. Max's dark pubic hair was gone.

Startled, Crane lifted his eyes and saw that Max's belly

and chest were equally bare. Even his arms and legs were hairless. Shaking his head slowly, Crane swallowed and met Max's amused gaze.

"What did you do?" he asked, breathless. His skin prickled from the heat rising in his chest—the blood roaring in his ears sounded like a waterfall.

Biting his bottom lip, Max ducked his head and looked up at Crane again with big eyes, the perfect coquette. "I went for a full body wax."

"Why?" It was barely a whisper.

He was a starved man staring at a feast—his mouth literally watered. Max had been similarly hairless the day he'd broken Crane out of prison, and the memory of his smooth, pliant nakedness in his hands that damning day was one that he'd returned to often.

Max turned in place slowly, revealing the bikini bottom was a thong, and Crane found he couldn't tear his eyes away from the thin pink string disappearing between the tanned moons of Max's ass.

"I did it for *you*, silly," Max said, peeking coyly over his shoulder at Crane. "Because you're feeling better." He put his hands behind him. "Since you liked it *so* very much when I did it last time. Oh, and *here*—an added surprise." Bending over, Max pulled his ass cheeks apart.

Gaping at the sparkling pink gem Max had unveiled, Crane was so turned on that he felt flushed and dizzy, like he was once more in the grip of a fever. He reached for Max with one hand while simultaneously tugging down his shorts with the other, and Max giggled as Crane pulled him back against him. Then, leaning forward to grasp the top of the balustrade, Max gave Crane another sly, backwards glance.

"Are you going to fuck me, Doc?" Max murmured, grinding his ass against Crane's throbbing cock. He went up on his toes and popped his hips up and back, wedging Crane's stiff shaft between his cheeks. Crane could feel the hard gem press into the underside of his cock. "Are you going to fuck my smooth pink hole with your big . . . hard . . . dick?" Max emphasized his words with three slow hip thrusts back into Crane's groin.

Clenching his jaw, Crane stared down at the throngs of beachgoers passing below their balcony. The railings were simple concrete slabs, so the two of them were only visible from the waist up, but it wouldn't take a genius to figure out what was happening if someone looked their way. He flared his nostrils and breathed deep, trying to slow his pulse, and took a step back.

Max let out a little sigh of disappointment, then reached back again, this time to grasp the sparkly gem. "Pleeaaaase, Doc?" he said in a teasing, little-boy voice. "Please fuck me?"

Crane stared in rapt silence as Max began pulling the toy out, his sphincter bulging before his hole slowly opened to birth a surprisingly thick silver plug. Max whimpered as it popped free, his slack hole glistening with lube, and the worry of onlookers was blown clear out of Crane's head as the thong slid back into place, bridging the dark-pink opening of Max's well-primed hole like a string on a guitar.

Fuck it.

Jerked forward by his eager cock, he tore the bikini aside to ram himself deep into Max, groaning as Max's slick insides gripped his entire length.

Despite letting out a quiet *ow*, Max pushed himself eagerly back into Crane's thrusts, bracing himself on the concrete railing so Crane's fervour didn't send them flying over the side.

Moaning, Max let his head fall forward, and Crane tightened his grip on the young man's hips, fucking him fast and hard. His balls were already tight with his imminent climax, but he wanted to delay it a little longer, so he turned his attention to the boardwalk to distract himself . . . and met the gaze of a familiar figure.

Crane stilled, his chest heaving. So, the large man in the too-small fedora *wasn't* one of his hallucinations?

"*Jesus*, Doc, don't stop now," Max said, sounding breathless.

Ignoring Max's soft mewl of protest when he pulled out, Crane stepped back from the balcony's edge, dragging Max after him. He shoved Max into the condo and hastily closed and locked the door behind them.

Who was the man? Police? And if so . . . why was he just watching them? What was he waiting for? Crane took a big step back from the patio door, the questions clawing through his mind like a trapped rat.

"What the hell?" Max sounded annoyed, but when Crane turned to him, his eyebrows popped up. "Are you all right? You look like you've seen a ghost."

Wiping his mouth with the back of his hand, Crane glanced back at the patio door and shook his head. "Uh. I . . . maybe. I don't know. It's probably nothing." Max would only tell him he was paranoid again. "Yeah, it's fine."

"Oh . . . *kay*," Max replied, not sounding convinced. Then he grinned and cocked his head, holding the jewelled plug up. "So, you gonna finish what you started, or am I going to have to make do with this?"

Either the bikini bottom had loosened from Crane's manhandling, or it was the way Max was standing, but a little more of Max's dick was on display, and the sight of it renewed Crane's flagging erection. It always confused him, this visceral reaction to Max's body. He'd never felt any sort of same-sex attraction before Max and couldn't think of a single instance of attraction to any man since—well, at least sober, if Max was to be believed.

Hell, he couldn't remember ever having felt this way about his wife's body.

No, it was just . . . Max.

All he had to do to make Crane's head swim with lust was put on a tight dress. But panties were Crane's favourite. Lacy or sheer enough that Crane could *see* Max through the fabric, Crane got so hard he could bend steel with his dick. But now it seemed a tiny thong bikini was the forerunner in Crane's long list of weaknesses where the young man was concerned. He let out a shuddering breath, the stranger on the boardwalk forgotten.

Crane plucked the jewelled plug from Max's hand. "Turn around and bend over," he growled.

Max did as he was told, with one hand on the back of the couch for balance, then squealed when Crane touched his pucker with the plug.

"Oh, that's *cold*." Max laughed, then sucked a breath through his teeth as Crane shoved the plug into his ass. "*Huhh*. Sadist."

Crane smirked. "You love it." He tilted his head and tugged on the plug to pull it out about halfway. When he let go, Max's ass immediately sucked it back in—Crane did it a few more times as he jerked himself, completely spellbound.

"Hey . . . Doc . . . this is nice and all, but I'd *really* like you to fuck me now, please and thank you."

Snapping out of his daze, Crane slapped Max's ass hard before pulling him up by his hair and pushing him forward into the far wall.

"Didn't say I was done with you."

Leaning into Max, he bent his knees so he was low enough to slide his dick between Max's smooth thighs. Max gasped and went up on his toes to accommodate Crane, arching his head back to rest it on Crane's shoulder as Crane's shaft rubbed the silky pink fabric, cupping Max's balls.

"Christ, why are you being such a fucking tease?" Max said after only a few seconds, sounding impatient. He squeezed his thighs together hard to trap Crane's cock between them. "I told you I want full-hilt Doc cock, not some half-assed bullsh—"

Crane's hand closed around the front of Max's throat to cut off his whining, then pushed up the bikini top to crush Max's nipple between thumb and finger.

Max let out a strangled cry, grappling at the hand at his throat, but Crane just laughed and kissed the side of Max's neck.

"If you really want me to fuck you good and hard, we're going to have to do something about that smart mouth of yours first," he murmured against Max's skin. "Now, go be a good boy and lie down on the bed." Max let out a raspy wail when Crane gave his nipple another punishing twist, but he nodded his head quickly, so Crane freed him.

With a sulky glare in Crane's direction, Max went to the bedroom, then threw himself face down on the bed with his legs hanging off the side.

"Like this?" he said, his voice muffled by the bedding. He wiggled his ass back and forth, making the pink gem twinkle.

Crane crawled onto the bed, the old spring mattress squeaking and chiming loudly in protest as Crane dragged Max to the middle and turned him over.

Max's dark brows came together as he stared up at Crane, but then he let out a sigh and smiled as Crane stroked his hand up his thigh, skirting the satiny pink bulge to run his hand over Max's tanned belly and up to his pecs where he gently pinched his reddened nipple.

"Mmm." Max arched his back as Crane stroked downward again along his chest and abs just to feel the smoothness against his palm. Then Crane paused, fingertips resting *just* above the bikini bottom, and he smiled, teasing Max by skimming his fingers gently back and forth along the line of fabric.

"*T'es mechant, mon amour*," Max whispered, closing his eyes as Crane feathered the softest of touches over his covered cock. "Why are you being so mean?"

Ignoring him, Crane shifted in place to go up on his knees so he was over Max's head, using both hands now to stroke him from the top of his naked groin to the small nipples perking up from the pale triangles of untanned skin. Max lifted himself to nuzzle Crane's balls, his tongue darting out to lick the base of his shaft, and Crane shut his eyes for a moment, just enjoying the feeling.

It didn't take long before his dick was drooling all over Max's chest, which gave him an idea. He carefully slid the bikini top back into place, covering up Max's nipples, but then dripped precum directly onto the pink triangles.

Mary had accidentally bought a bikini once that went

transparent when wet—Crane was pleased to see that Max's bikini had the same "flaw" when the darker peaks of Max's stiff nipples became visible through the thin fabric. Crane's cock throbbed in his fist, and he had to stop stroking himself for a moment for fear of blowing his load already.

"Jesus," he whispered, breathing heavily, then gasped when Max's tongue ventured to his asshole. He jerked up higher on his knees. "Don't do that." Crane just couldn't get comfortable with Max doing . . . *that*.

"Why not?" Max grabbed Crane by the hips, trying to pull him back down to tongue his hole again, but Crane crawled backwards and dropped down on all fours to feed Max his cock instead.

Closing his mouth around Crane eagerly, Max hummed around the shaft as Crane gave a few shallow thrusts. Max's dick was slowly hardening right before Crane's eyes, eventually escaping its pink spandex confines. It poked obscenely from the side of the bikini bottom, stiff and veiny, the dusky, bulbous head just beginning to emerge from the pale collar of foreskin.

Staring at Max's naked erection, Crane clenched his jaw. He'd taken Max into his mouth before, a few times now, in fact, but only ever while in the warm, hazy grip of alcohol or drugs—he had no recollection of doing it.

Liar.

He blinked and averted his gaze, disconcerted by the vivid mental image of easing himself down on his elbows to reach Max's cock with his mouth. Was it a memory, or was it a desire?

I came in your mouth, you know, Max had said after showing him those pictures so long ago. *And you swallowed.*

The voice inside him was right. He *was* a liar. He did remember it—the hard, thin-skinned shaft, hot between his lips. The glossy smooth head . . . he *knew* what Max tasted like.

Crane bared his teeth and started fucking Max's mouth a little harder until Max gagged, flailing against him to push him off, but Crane grabbed one of Max's wrists to stop him, forcing it down by Max's side before capturing the other, using his weight to pin Max's arms to the mattress while he pushed himself hard into Max's throat. Again, Max struggled in vain, his heels drumming the mattress as Crane continued to fuck his mouth deep and slow.

He wasn't even angry or averse to sucking Max's dick. Not anymore, anyway. They were well past that, and even Crane had to admit his continued shows of resistance towards actively participating in certain things were starting to seem . . . forced.

It was just that for Max, everything was about coercion and power, and going down on him now, stone-cold sober as he was, would be taken as some twisted victory over him, and Crane couldn't afford to lose what tiny bit of control he still had in their relationship.

In fact, if Max's brain had been wired like a decent fucking human being's, Crane *would* have gone ahead and sucked him off . . . but, that was the problem, wasn't it? Max being wired any other way wouldn't be Max, and Crane would never have been attracted to him in the first place and thus wouldn't be here, on the run in a foreign country with a price on his head, his dick lodged deep in Max's throat while he did mental gymnastics over reciprocating the blowjob. Shaking his head, he sighed.

Max twitched, and Crane suddenly realized he'd stopped trying to buck him off for some time now. Startled, he let go of Max's wrists and sat back. Thankfully, the second his dick left Max's mouth, Max sucked in a ragged breath and sat up, clutching at his throat as he coughed and wheezed, tears running down his face. Crane watched him for a few seconds, relieved that he hadn't gone too far.

Relieved or disappointed?

"I got distracted," he said weakly.

"You *think*?" Max rasped, glowering at him as he sat there hunched over, trying to catch his breath.

Crane realized something and frowned.

"You could have used your teeth."

Instantly, Max's cheeks dimpled in a bright grin, and he rubbed his face with his palms, wiping away the tears. "Baby, what would be the fun in *that*?" He popped up to his knees, thighs wide-open while he leaned back, adjusting the bikini so that his dick poked up above the fabric; then he cocked his head, bit his lip, and squeezed his nipple through the precum-damp triangle.

"So . . . did I earn a Dennis penis?" Max asked, using the French pronunciation of the word so it rhymed with his name: peh-niss. "Hm?" He slid his hand slowly down his chest as he pushed his pelvis out, making his cock twitch as he clenched internal muscles. A drip of precum rolled down the smooth head and naked shaft like a tear, wetting the pink fabric that still cradled his balls.

With a low growl, Crane pulled Max to him, kissing him deeply as he cupped his smooth backside in both hands, grinding their hard cocks together. Max moaned, raking Crane's back gently with his nails as he moved in his arms.

The boy was as pliant and soft and sensual as a nymph in a fairy tale.

"Come here," Crane murmured against Max's soft lips, pulling him down to the mattress.

He had Max lie on his side and curled up behind him, spooning him, then hooked his thumb under the thong to pull it aside while lifting Max's ass cheek. Then, breathing hard, he pushed himself gently into the smooth pink pucker—just a slow, slick plunge until he was fully seated inside Max, locking them in their embrace, bodies pressed together tight.

"*Huhh*," Max said, his thighs shuddering against Crane's. "Now *that's* more like it."

Crane brushed the curls from Max's nape to press his lips to it, then trailed his fingers from Max's shoulder to his knee, letting his touch wander on the way back up, crossing to the bikini bottom and the soft forms nestled within.

He felt more than heard Max's gasp when his fingertips skimmed higher, bumping from satiny fabric to skin to feather a touch up along the bottom of Max's cock. He smiled against Max's skin and moved his hand to Max's hip, where he deftly undid the little bow holding the bikini bottom together, letting the material fall away so he could fondle Max's hairless balls for a moment before wrapping his hand around the smooth, stiff shaft.

"Oh, *Doc*," came Max's needy little whisper, nudging his pelvis forward into Crane's gentle touch. He whimpered then moaned, surrendering to slow Crane's caresses.

Maybe Max isn't the only one who's in control.

Shutting his eyes, Crane began to move slowly, his hand stroking Max as he thrust into him.

Anyone looking in could have easily mistaken this for

lovemaking, but Crane recognized and accepted it for what it was. It was a defence mechanism. A coping strategy. A stalling technique. A cry for help.

Crane sighed.

Then why does it feel *like love?*

NINE
THE MAN AND HIS TINY HAT

Crane left a note for Max, letting him know he'd gone out for errands and closed the door quietly behind him so he wouldn't wake Max from his well-deserved nap. Whistling, he took the stairs down, spinning the key ring on his finger as he shielded his eyes against the midafternoon sun.

He stopped on the last step and stood there momentarily, just glad to be out of the house. It felt great. *He* felt great.

Crane watched a family of four cross the street, the mother squinting down at the phone in her hand while dragging along a little boy in bathing trunks. From the pallor of their skin, Crane assumed they'd just arrived and weren't familiar yet with the area. Sure enough, the father spotted Crane and steered the baby stroller towards him, a smile on his face.

"Howdy! Hablar Ang-lays?" the man asked in a twangy accent as he touched the rim of his cap.

"I do," Crane replied. "Are you looking for the beach?"

"We are," the man replied, then called to his wife. "Mags, I found help!"

Crane grinned. "Just keep following this road, then turn left at the fence. You'll see the access to the beach right away."

"Thank you. We got turned 'round," the man said, jiggling the stroller back and forth a few times to soothe its cranky occupant. "Much obliged. Mags, it's this way!"

Watching them go, Crane felt his mood shift. Soberly, he thought about how foreign it all seemed to him now. Just a nice little family vacation where no one was trying to drug or manipulate anyone, where no one had to worry about winding up in jail or whether someone was going to sodomize them while drunk . . .

Booooring.

With a rueful chuckle, Crane shook his head and went up the street in the opposite direction of the tourist family and had to admit the voice in his head had a point. If there was one thing life with Max certainly wasn't, it was *boring*.

The first stop was to the tiny post office a few blocks up from La Quinta, where Max had his mail delivered. It was always a little awkward to go there on his own because none of the people working there spoke much English, and it always took a few tries to get his point across, even with the little phrase guide he kept in his pocket.

Thankfully, today it went smoothly, and mood buoyed once more, Crane flipped through the mail—mostly letters forwarded to Mexico from Max's ringer in Paris—as he took a side street to a liquor store where he wouldn't have to pay tourist prices for Max's tequila.

Crane grinned. For the pink bikini stunt, he decided to splurge and buy top-shelf for his *not*-boring partner.

Partner? Crane furrowed his brow, his pace slowing. *Boyfriend? Lover?* None of those fit.

He blinked and lifted his head, skin prickling with the feeling that someone was watching him. Glancing around, Crane didn't see anything suspicious, but a few steps later, he saw a flash of bright green out of the corner of his eye, and his heart stilled. The man on the boardwalk had been wearing a bright-green shirt. All thoughts of tequila vanished as Crane walked faster, taking the first left, then doubling back a block, then down to La Quinta where there were more tourists. He stopped in front of a store selling painted skulls, or *calaveras*, and pretended to browse.

Sure enough, only a minute or two passed before Crane spotted the large man in the small hat reflected in the shop window.

Clenching his jaw, he debated sprinting back to the safety of the condo. But how safe was that if the man obviously knew where they lived?

No, he'd get to the bottom of this now. He straightened, his heart beating so hard it felt like he couldn't take a full breath, and slowly turned around.

Crane deliberately met the man's gaze, not blinking as he closed the gap between them.

He glared down at his stalker. "Why are you following me?"

"Please, lower your voice." The man looked nervously from side to side. "Not here. Come . . . let me buy you a drink. We need to talk."

His Spanish accent was pronounced, but he was obviously comfortable speaking English. Crane had no problem understanding him.

"I'm not going anywhere until you tell me who you are."

The man's bushy black brows pinched together above his

nose, and he cleared his throat. "I am someone who needs your help, Dr. Crane. And someone who can offer help in return."

Crane felt a little faint. The man knew who he was. "What kind of help?"

"How would you like to clear your name?"

○

Crane stared wide-eyed at the man seated across from him in the hotel bar and clenched his hands beneath the small round table.

"You want me to help you take down a *Mexican cartel?*" he said slowly.

Inspector López shrugged and pushed sweat-damp hair back off his forehead.

"That's the gist, yes," the *Federale* replied, fiddling with the brim of the undersized fedora he'd balanced on his knee. "And in doing so, all charges against you will be dropped, and your escape from prison pardoned."

Working with the Canadian and American governments, the Mexican government had created a special joint task force to fight cross-border drug smuggling, specifically targeting the cartel responsible for the designer drug Max had dosed him with. Unbeknownst to Crane, Max had been working for the Luján cartel for weeks . . . because, of *course* he was. What kind of courier job involved paper bags full of American money? He was stupid not to have questioned it.

Crane pinched the bridge of his nose, trying to wrap his brain around what López was asking of him.

"So, this meeting that's happening with the head of the Luhar . . ."

"Luján."

"Thank you. So, this meeting is happening sometime in the next week, and you want me to be there with Max and Preston while they do some sort of deal to smuggle that *víbora* drug into the US and Canada using Preston's yacht?"

"Yes," López replied, lifting his hand to catch the eye of their waitress. She came over with a smile, and he started ordering in Spanish but paused and looked to Crane. "Another?"

Crane had downed the first Dos Equis quickly and already felt a little buzzed, but the alcohol was calming his nerves, so he nodded.

"But how is that going to clear my name?" He was so confused.

"Once we have Édouard, or *Max*, I should say, in custody and he is extradited to Canada, he will be tried for fabricating and tampering with evidence in your trial. Some troubling things came to light about your . . . ah . . . *friend* these past months. Links to several crime syndicates. Some very shady dealings." López clicked his tongue twice, shaking his head.

"And I can't just . . . hand him over to you and go back to Canada a free man? You need me to get involved in this drug business first?"

"Yes." López thanked the waitress for his beer and took a long pull from the bottle, ignoring the fresh glass she had brought. "It'll . . . how do you say? Grease the wheels? Is that the expression?"

"Yeah."

"Instead of waiting for months for all the red tape, your

record will be"—he lifted his hand and opened his fist quickly —"*poof*. Gone."

Crane took a sip of his beer, pondering. It sounded convoluted and dangerous, but more than that . . . could he really be free of Max? Did he *want* to be free of him? He thought about how nice the last week had been and felt his stomach twist. Was it fear? Guilt? Hope?

"And this is why you've been stalking me? Why didn't you approach me earlier?"

"I was waiting for the right time. I didn't want to spook you."

"Yeah. Good job on that, buddy," Crane muttered before taking another swig of beer. "I need some time to think about it."

"No. If you don't do as I ask, I will simply arrest you and send you back to Canada. Yes, they'll eventually sort out the details of *Señor* Duvernay's involvement in the crimes you're innocent of, but you're still facing what . . . ten years for breaking out of prison?" López shrugged good-naturedly.

Scowling, Crane sat back. "So . . . it's extortion then? If I don't play nice, you make sure I get good and screwed?"

"Ah, don't be that way, Dr. Crane. Don't you want to help? Be a hero?" López said, a sunny smile dimpling his cheeks. "These drugs are very, very bad, my friend. And it's not just *la víbora*. There is a second drug—*la araña*—that is worse."

"Worse than *víbora*? Jesus. Is that even possible?"

"No, ah . . . not worse in the intoxication sense. It's similar to *la víbora* in that it makes the individual *extremely* open to suggestion . . . but without the high feeling."

"Huh." Crane frowned. "Why would anyone want to take that for fun?"

"Think of it this way: what would a terrorist group do with a drug that could make someone do *anything* they want? What if they had enough to put it in . . . say, a city water supply? They could cause massive chaos."

Crane nodded. The man had a point . . . but it all sounded an awful lot like the plot of a movie he'd seen before. But which one?

"What about Max? What happens to him?"

The *Federale* blew air through his generous lips. "It's over for him. He'll be a very old man by the time he breathes fresh air again." López narrowed his eyes at Crane. "Don't you want to see him pay for what he has done to you, my friend?"

Crane chuckled nervously under the intense gaze of the Mexican cop. "Well . . . yes. Of *course*. He ruined my life."

"Then it is settled." López pulled a box out of his pocket along with a small roll of white tape. "This is for you."

When Crane opened the cardboard box, he found a thin silver wire wrapped around a coin-sized square of black plastic nestled inside. He blinked at it a few times, then raised his eyes to López.

"What is it?"

"A microphone and ah . . . how do you say? Audio capture? Recorder?"

Crane felt the sweat trickle down his back as he looked down in alarm at the device in the box.

"You want me to wear a *wire*?" he said in a hoarse whisper. His heart was pounding so hard he felt dizzy.

"Yes."

Wiping his palms on his shorts, Crane breathed deeply, trying to calm himself.

"I don't know know if I can . . ."

"It's up to you, Dr. Crane. Wear the wire or . . . how do you say? Wear striped pyjamas?" López chuckled to himself, then reached out and tilted the neck of his beer bottle towards Crane. "So? Do we have a deal?"

He could be a free man. Free to live his life . . . free from Max.

Is that what you really *want, Doc? Hm?*

Licking his lips, Crane held out his beer with a shaky hand and clinked it against Inspector López's, his stomach twisting in knots.

It's just Stockholm syndrome. The guilt I feel is misplaced. Max absolutely deserves everything he has coming to him. I can do this. I have to do this.

"Deal," he heard himself say in a weak voice.

"Good." The *Federale* gave him a firm nod followed by a sympathetic smile. "You look like you need another beer."

"Yes." Crane cleared his throat, trying to ignore the tendrils of panic winding their way up through his chest to choke him. "Please."

Crane opened the door to the condo and walked across to the kitchen island a little unsteadily. He set down the mail and the shopping bags, then gasped and went rigid when arms slid around him from behind.

"Hey, darling." Max slid his cool hands up under Crane's loose shirt to caress him as he kissed the back of his shoulder.

"You startled me." Hyperconscious of the small box in his

front pocket, Crane's breath hitched as Max's fingertips suddenly ventured downwards. He quickly turned around and took Max by the shoulders, pecking a quick kiss on his lips. "Hang on. I have to use the bathroom."

Max frowned up at him. "You smell like beer."

"Uh. Yeah. I, um, was waiting for them to make a fresh batch of churros, so I had a beer while I . . . waited." He winced inwardly at his awkwardness. "You know, at the little bar next to the churro place?"

"Fresh churros?" Max's eyes had lit up at his words making Crane instantly regret his lie.

Max reached for the shopping bag, so Crane hastily added, "But, they were taking so long that I figured I'd come back here and we could go down together. You know, go for a walk? We haven't taken a walk together in a while." He knew he was babbling, but he couldn't stop.

"You're acting weird."

"Am I?" Crane chuckled self-consciously.

Max tilted his head, his eyes flat and reptilian as he stared at Crane for a long moment. Then he broke out into a wide grin.

"That pretty girl was tending bar again, eh? What's her name . . . Adelina?" Max bit his bottom lip, his expression sly. "Was she aggressively flirting with you like last time?"

Crane let out a quiet sigh of relief and nodded, trying to look sheepish.

"Yeah, and just . . . I dunno. I know she's just doing it for the tips, but it makes me so uncomfortable. I finished my beer too quickly, and I guess I just forgot about the churros." He gave Max a contrite smile. "I'm sorry. I'm a little tipsy."

"Aw, that's okay, Doc. I could use the walk. Hang on." Max left the room to put on some clothes.

Crane sagged against the kitchen island, cursing to himself, one hand over the square lump in his pocket. He quickly straightened when Max reappeared only a few moments later, already clothed. He had a bag in one hand.

"Hey, I had a thought . . . why don't we go to the Mayakoba and use that day pass Preston and Viv gave us? I grabbed our swim trunks—I hear the swimming pools there are primo." Max gave Crane a coy smile. "Maybe we can book a little couples massage too while we're there?"

Grinning, Crane nodded, glad that Max's focus had shifted away from him. "Sure, let's go." He took a step towards the door.

"I thought you had to use the bathroom."

He turned back to Max in time to see suspicion flit across his face before a bland smile replaced it. "Right! One sec. Gotta pee." Crane walked as nonchalantly as he could to the bathroom, then stood there staring at himself wide-eyed in the mirror.

"Get it together, you fucking idiot," he whispered to his reflection. First, he needed to hide the wire where Max wouldn't find it. Next, he had to figure out some way of getting invited to this meeting with Jorge "El Lobo" Morales, the leader of the Luján cartel. How the fuck was he going to do that?

"I have to go to the Mayakoba to see Preston, anyway," Max called out from the other side of the door.

"Oh, yeah?" Crane fished the box and little roll of tape out of his pocket, reaching up to place them quietly on top of the bathroom mirror. He took a step back, then crouched down to Max's height, making sure he couldn't see the box, then quickly used the toilet. "Why?"

"One of the guys I work for, Señor Morales, invited me to this barbecue thing on Friday and he asked me to bring Preston." Max's voice was very clear—it sounded like he was leaning right against the door. Was he checking to see if Crane actually needed to use the bathroom? Did he suspect something?

"Oh, yeah?" Crane glanced up at the hidden wire again as he washed his hands and hastily dried them on the towel.

Max looked up at Crane when he opened the door, his expression neutral. "Yeah."

"A barbecue . . . uh, that sounds fun."

"I guess," Max replied, wrinkling his nose. "It would be more fun if you were there. Wanna come? I'm sure it'll be fine."

And just like that, Crane was in. He shoved his hands in his pockets and pretended to mull it over, trying to quell his nerves.

Max doesn't know. He can't know, can he?

"Sure. Why not?"

Beaming, Max went up on tiptoe to give Crane a soft, lingering kiss, and Crane couldn't tell which was worse: his breathless paranoia or his crippling guilt.

Max broke away with a smirk, then put his hands together like he was praying. "Okay, can we *pleaaaase* go now? I *need* a churro and a swim, *stat*."

Crane gave a little laugh, forcing himself to relax, and reached out to lift the hem of Max's T-shirt.

"What are you going to do about this?" he asked, exposing

the crisp white outlines of the micro bikini on Max's bronzed chest.

"What do you mean?" Max's smile slowly dimpled one cheek. "Are you worried about the dirty old men that are going to stare at me? Or are *you* the dirty old man who's going to be staring at me, and you're worried that everyone will see your boner?"

"Maybe both?" Crane rubbed his thumb over one of Max's perky little nipples, making it harder. Chuckling, he then tweaked it and Max let out a gasp. Shit, his dick *was* getting hard. "Maybe we should stay home for a little bit first. You know . . . just to be on the safe side."

"Oh, yeah?" Max licked his lips, cupping the stiffening bulge in Crane's shorts. "Maybe that *is* a good idea."

"Hmm." Crane closed his eyes and tilted his head back, enjoying Max's touch.

"But it's gotta be lickety-split, wham-bam-*thank*-you-man fast."

"Mmhm." He let out a shuddering sigh as his zipper came down.

"Because I really *do* need to talk to Preston about Friday."

"Uh-huh." Crane groaned as Max pulled his dick out, but then his words finally registered, and Crane's anxiety came back in a rush.

Right. The meeting with the cartel where he was going to betray Max to the authorities.

Crane opened his eyes and met Max's upturned gaze, unnerved by the little pensive comma between his dark brows. He cleared his throat, ignoring the lead ball in his gut, and used his thumb to pull Max's bottom lip down, opening his mouth.

"Well? What the fuck are you waiting for? Get down on your fucking knees and suck my cock."

Max's forehead wrinkled up, and he grinned, licking the tip of Crane's thumb before dropping to his knees right there in the bathroom doorway.

Crane's eyes strayed to the top of the mirror again before he crushed them closed, trying to focus on Max's hot, wet mouth.

After all, how many times did they have left together before everything was over?

TEN

THE PLEASANT BARBECUE WHERE
NOTHING BAD COULD POSSIBLY
HAPPEN

FRIDAY, DECEMBER 1ST

"What's wrong?"

Crane blinked, turning away from the cab's window, and had to swallow back the lump of anxiety before answering. "Wrong? What do you mean?"

"You're like . . . drenched."

Looking down, Crane grimaced. His shirt was splotched where it was stuck to his sweaty chest. "Oh. Yeah. I guess I didn't realize how hot it was going to be today," he lied. The fabric tape López had provided was white, and though the *Federale* had assured Crane that it would go unnoticed no matter what colour shirt he wore, he'd decided to go with his white dress shirt, despite the long sleeves.

Following López's instructions, he'd carefully secured the tiny microphone and wire along the inside seam of the front placket with the small recorder taped behind the bottom button. Crane had been surprised that he wasn't supposed to secure the microphone to his chest the way they did it in the movies, but it made sense that if he were frisked and asked to open or lift his shirt, the wire would remain hidden.

"I don't get why you needed to get all fancy." Max was wearing a worn dark-blue T-shirt with *Safari Inn* across the chest in a vintage-looking yellow font and grey shorts. "I told you it wasn't formal."

"Well . . . I don't know. I'm not used to meeting people of such . . . ah, *prominence*."

Max made a face. "Señor Morales is just a businessman, you dork."

"Uh-huh," Crane replied, looking away.

Max had told him that Jorge Morales was the CEO and owner of Farmacéuticos Luján, a big pharmaceutical company based out of Quintana Roo. It was odd that Max was lying about who his boss really was, but maybe "El Lobo" had told him to keep Crane in the dark about the Luján cartel. Or, maybe Max was just lying because he was Max.

Or . . . Crane glanced back at Max who gave him a reassuring smile and squeezed his thigh gently. Could it be that Max didn't want to worry him?

Yeah, right.

Crane returned Max's smile as another trickle of sweat slid down his chest. He was sweating because he was nervous, but it *was* also hot out.

"I'll roll up my sleeves then," he said, unbuttoning his left cuff.

"Atta boy." Max watched him fix his sleeves, then reached for his collar.

Crane froze, his pulse soaring as Max deftly undid the top button.

"That's better, Doc?"

"Yes," Crane replied in a faint voice. He wanted to look down to see if the microphone was visible but forced himself to stay still as Max tousled his hair.

"There. Now you look a little less like you got a stick up your rear."

Crane snorted in amusement despite his nerves. "Thanks."

"Don't worry." Max looked up at him endearingly. "I'm sure you two will get along like a house on fire."

"Okay." Crane turned away, taking a quick peek down at his collar to reassure himself the wire was still hidden before going back to staring out at the passing buildings and foliage. He spent the rest of the hour's drive from Playa del Carmen to Tulum, sweating quietly and hoping the microphone was waterproof.

While Max paid the cabbie, Crane stood frowning up at the modern white townhouse nestled within a large manicured garden.

This was not what he'd expected at all. Weren't cartel bosses supposed to live in big compounds surrounded by high walls? Where were the armed henchmen? Where was the barbed wire? He stepped out of the way of a well-dressed woman walking a little brown and white dog along the edge of the street, then looked around at the neighbouring townhouses. It was all very upper-class suburbia.

"You okay?"

Startled, Crane turned to Max. "Um. Yes. Are we at the right place?"

"Yeah. I've been here plenty of times." Max tilted his head. "Why?"

"I just assumed that a . . . *CEO*"—he paused to give Max an indulgent smile—"would live somewhere more . . . secure."

Max's eyebrows rose slowly as he gazed at Crane. "Why are you acting so gosh darn *weird*? I swear you've been off all week. Baby, is there something you want to tell me?"

Crane quickly shook his head. "No." *Yes. I'm about to hand you over to the feds to save myself.* "Should we wait for Preston before going in? Where is he anyway?" he asked, changing the subject.

Max shrugged. "He was dying to come. It wouldn't surprise me if he was already here. Shall we?" Max passed his arm through Crane's and gestured to the walkway.

Steeling himself, Crane nodded, and they walked to the red-stained wood door where Max used the heavy knocker to signal their arrival. A few moments later, the door opened.

"Come. Come in." The smiling man at the door was trim and handsome, with black wavy hair that had gone bright silver at the temples, a narrow, well-shaped nose, and a black handlebar moustache. He was wearing a tropical shirt covered in colourful fish, a pair of off-white trousers, and on his feet were a pair of brown woven-leather sandals. He was a very oddly dressed guard or henchman, but maybe that was to put El Lobo's guests at ease.

Crane stepped in and raised his arms for the expected pat down but was met with quizzical looks from Max and the man who'd opened the door.

"What are you *doing*?" Max asked.

Red-faced, Crane dropped his arms. "Ah, it was a long car ride." He cleared his throat. "Just stretching."

Shaking his head, Max turned to the man in the tropical shirt. "Forgive him, Señor Morales. I think the heat is getting to him."

Shit.

Crane stared at their host, hastily putting his hand out. "Pleased to meet you. Denni—" He cleared his throat to cover his mistake. "*Dan has* told me, uh, so much about you. I'm Robert . . . Rob."

Morales shook with Crane, his palm cool and dry against Crane's sweat-damp one. "Jorge Morales. Please, call me Jorge. Why *conejito* here insists on calling me *Señor*, I'll never understand."

Crane felt a frown flicker across his face at what he took to be a term of endearment, judging by the fondness in Morales's voice. His suspicions deepened when the man placed a possessive hand on Max's shoulder as the two had a brief, amiable exchange in Spanish.

Schooling his features, Crane tried in vain to ignore the high-definition image searing his brain in lurid technicolour detail—one of Max spreading his thighs for the dashing Morales.

Why the hell do you *care who he's fucking? You're about to sell him out to the feds.* Crane flared his nostrils, trying to ignore the voice in his head. *Traitor.*

"Let's go to the living room." The corners of Morales's charming smile disappeared into his moustache as he looked from Max to Crane. "It's nice and cool inside."

"Thank you." Crane was startled when Max took his hand. "Uh . . ." He looked to their host, but the man had his back to them.

"He knows you're my paramour, *mi amor*, and doesn't

139

give a fig," Max said before pressing a kiss to the back of Crane's hand. He pulled a face. "Ugh. You're *so* sweaty."

"Sorry. I'll try to sweat less."

Morales led them to a large white-walled living room with terracotta tiled floors and high ceilings. Atop a colourful woven rug sat three comfortable-looking oxblood leather couches and a carved, round wooden coffee table with a ceramic bowl of fruit at its centre. The walls were adorned with bright paintings and woven pieces of art. Stairs led to a second-floor gallery with a balustrade in the same red-stained wood as the front door. Off the living room, a double set of glass doors looked out onto a patio with a huge kidney-shaped pool surrounded by potted tropical plants and white loungers.

Crane heard voices and turned as a tall man dressed in black came up the hallway, speaking in Spanish to someone behind him. Shaved to the skin, his head glinted in the overhead light as he walked towards them. He had a thin, angular goatee that framed a hard mouth, thick bushy, dark brows that met in the middle over a sharp hawk nose, and piercing green eyes. The only parts of his outfit that weren't solid black were the silver cow's skull clasp on his bolo tie and the metal tips on his pointy-toed cowboy boots.

"Ah . . . and here is my brother Carlos. Carlos, this is Robert," Morales said.

So, this was Carlos "El Verdugo" Espada, Morales's half-brother. Inspector López had explained that while Morales was the head of the cartel, Espada was the fist. He certainly looked the part.

Crane held out his hand nervously and was startled when Espada grabbed it and slapped his shoulder hard as he vigorously shook his hand. The smile that had appeared on the tall man's face was such a contrast to his intimidating appearance that Crane was distracted and didn't notice who else had entered the room.

"And this is my favourite niece, Gabriela," added Morales.

Turning, Crane could only blink stupidly at the young woman for a moment.

"Nice to meet you, Robert." Her voice was soft and lilting, and her tone was demure—the picture of sweet innocence . . . until she gave him a sly wink.

There was no mistaking it. This was the young woman Max had been fooling around with at the condo. The one that had passed out or nearly so while he . . .

Oh my god.

Not trusting his voice, Crane swallowed hard and smiled, nodding at her politely. He could see her perky little breasts in his mind's eye and remembered her scent lingering in their bedroom. Turning to Max, Crane knew immediately that Espada and Morales were clueless about what Max had been up to with the girl. Though Max's smile was blandly cordial, mischief danced in his eyes.

Crane stared hard at Max for a beat, wishing he could drag him into another room to ask him *what the fuck* he was thinking, messing around with her, but he forced himself to take a deep, calming breath and turned back to their host.

"You have a lovely home," he said, his voice a little unsteady. A bead of sweat trickled down his chest, making him itchy, but he resisted the urge to scratch for fear of dislodging the microphone. "That's some . . . ah, beautiful artwork." He gestured to the walls.

"Thank you! Would you like a tour?"

"Oh, yes, please." Even though it was the last thing in the world Crane wanted to do, it seemed unwise to refuse.

What he *did* want was for someone to say something incriminating about drugs and the deal with Preston and his yacht and then find an excuse to get the hell out of there.

So that you can throw me under the bus, right, Doc?

Crane glanced over at Max who smiled fondly at him.

"Yeah, go on, honey. I've seen it all before," Max said brightly as he turned to leave. "I'll go make some drinks for everyone."

"*Mi vida*," Morales said, beckoning to his niece. He put his arm around her waist and pulled her in for a kiss on the temple. On the surface, it was a sweet, avuncular display, but then Gabriela flinched. It was just a brief, nearly imperceptible change in expression, but it spoke volumes. "Gabriela, please go help Dan with the drinks?" Crane saw that Morales's hand had slid down to rest lecherously close to the young woman's backside.

"Yes, *tío*," she replied softly.

Keeping his expression neutral despite his revulsion, Crane met Gabriela's eye and saw the shame and anger simmering beneath her pleasant smile.

"That's a good girl." Morales actually patted her on the rump to send her away, seemingly oblivious to the dark look that had flashed across his half-brother's face when he did it. "All right. *Vamos*." Morales clapped Crane on the back. "This way."

The townhouse had many rooms, most of which had no function other than to store Morales's vast collection of art and artifacts. As Morales led Crane from one treasure room to the next, Crane cleared his throat and decided to ask the questions that were gnawing at him.

"Is there a *Mrs.* Morales?"

Morales stopped and turned to him, an affable smile on his moustachioed face. "No. Not yet. Perhaps one day." He shrugged. "Thankfully, I have my Gabriela to keep me company."

It was an effort to keep the disgust off his face. "You two seem very close," Crane said, keeping his tone light.

"Yes! She is my little darling. Isn't she beautiful?" Morales gave Crane another broad smile when he nodded. "I don't know what I would do without her. Whenever she speaks of going off to travel the world, I ask, 'Why? You have everything you could wish for here!' and I tell her that her poor *tío* would die of a broken heart if she left me."

"Ah." Crane frowned in a way he hoped conveyed the illusion of sympathy. "Surely that's not for a while yet? She seems so young."

"She only *looks* young. She takes after her mother, Julieta." Morales gestured for Crane to take the door to his right.

"Oh, yeah?"

"Julieta is a great beauty too. She and I . . . well, let's just say that she and I were close once. Before Carlos." He gave Crane a sly smile. "This was when she was about Gabriela's age."

"Which is . . .?" Crane asked, unable to keep from digging.

At Crane's question, the man's hospitable demeanour disappeared, his expression changing so dramatically that Crane took a half step back.

"Why do you want to know so much about my niece?" Eyes narrowed menacingly, Morales curled his lip as he stared up at Crane.

"I, uh . . . I'm just making conversation." Crane laughed nervously, wondering why he was doing his best to piss off a cartel boss—the man obviously had a hair-trigger temper. His pulse thudded dully in his ears as he lifted his hands in supplication. "I have no interest in your niece. Trust me. I have Ma— uh, my Dan."

Morales's expression mellowed, and he nodded.

"Ah, yes," he said, and his lips slowly curved into a suggestive smirk as he stared up at Crane. "Daniel. He *is* quite something."

The image of Max and Morales together flashed back into Crane's brain, front and centre, and his stomach clenched in response. He breathed slowly through his nose, his hands fisted by his sides.

"He is," Crane replied tersely.

"I never understood the appeal, you know. Of men together." Morales shook his head with a little grimace, then his expression went coy. "But a pretty young man like Daniel has a certain *way* about him, doesn't he?" When he winked, the implications were clear.

Crane saw red, his blood boiling with blind, gut-churning rage. Had they been in the room containing Morales's trove of antique swords, he would have grabbed one to run the man through without a second thought. Instead, he blinked and froze before his fists acted on their own, amazed by his urge to beat the man to death with his bare hands—something that undoubtedly would get *him* killed in the process.

In those few tense freeze-frame seconds, Crane realized

he couldn't go through with Inspector López's plan. Not if he was willing to murder a man for just *insinuating* that he had touched or *wanted* to touch Max. Sending Max to prison where he'd be surrounded by dozens of men who would no doubt want their fill of him? Crane would never survive it. Like it or not, his addiction was incurable.

Well . . . so much for clearing my name.

He and Max would just have to keep running from the law as long as they could. Together.

Putting his fury in check, Crane felt his heart begin to slow as he accepted his decision. Already, he found he could breathe more deeply as the tension drained from his muscles. He straightened his spine and looked down to meet Morales's gaze unflinchingly, buoyed by the intense relief he felt now that he was no longer going to lose Max.

"He *is* special, isn't he?" Crane kept his tone polite but spoke slowly to ensure his warning was understood. "And he is *mine*."

Morales looked startled. The man was obviously not used to being talked to in such a way. For a moment, he seemed unsure how to respond.

Crane took Morales's silent bemusement as an opportunity to give him a broad, overly friendly smile.

"So, what's in this room?" he asked enthusiastically, as if the last few minutes hadn't happened, and looked around.

The room was painted a rich brick-red with art hanging on all four walls—to Crane's inexperienced eye, they all seemed to be works from the same artist—and the floor was carpeted in a lush Turkish-style rug. At the very centre of the room was a large glass box atop a gaudy gold pillar. Turning, Crane noticed a familiar painting across the room.

"Hey! I know this one. We have this exact same print hanging in our living room," he said, stepping closer to it. He tried to remember the name of it but came up blank. Something with an X. He stared hard at the dog-man creature and frowned as the remnants of a memory tickled the edges of his mind, just out of reach.

"That is no print," Morales said, standing next to Crane. The man had evidently decided to play along and ignore the tense exchange they'd just had, reprising his role as benign host, but there was an edge to his voice that hadn't been there before. "That is the original." He gestured to the other walls. "They all are paintings by the great María Natalia Robles."

"Ah. I see."

"This one is my personal favourite. It is *Xolotl* . . . the god of monsters."

How fitting.

"It's quite something." Crane glanced at Morales and saw the man was watching him intently, so he pointed to the display case in the middle of the room. "What's in there?"

"Come. This is most special," Morales replied, his smile becoming genuine as the pride over showing off his collection returned. "My most-prized possessions."

Curious, Crane followed Morales.

On top of a square of dark-blue velvet were five antique gold coins with uneven, brittle edges, their surfaces hand stamped with crosses, crowns, or shields.

Eyebrows high, Crane leaned closer for a better look. "Are these . . . doubloons? Like, Spanish Doubloons? Like the kind you see in pirate movies?"

Chuckling, Morales nodded. "Yes. Exactly that. These are so, *so* precious. They are from the 1715 Fleet shipwrecks. Do you know about it? No? Eleven ships went down in the same hurricane in 1715—the *Tierra Firme* and *Nueva España* fleets. They were carrying great treasure from the New World to Spain, and all was lost. Well . . . until some became found." Enthusiasm restored, Morales pointed to his collection. "See the little details here? And here? How they are imperfectly perfect? *Dios mío*, you can *feel* the history just by looking at them."

"Ah. I see. Yes." Crane peered down at the coins.

"You see that one in the middle?"

The coins were set in a square, with the largest coin sitting in the centre. It had an intricate shield on it.

"Yeah."

"That one is incredibly rare. It's called a *Tricentenario Real*. Only a handful have been found. Do you know how much that one is worth?"

"Ah . . . I really don't know anything about—"

"Guess." There was a gleam in Morales's eye. Sure, the man *felt* the history, but he obviously *loved* the richesse of his collection and enjoyed showing it off.

"I don't know. Um. A thousand dollars?"

Morales scoffed. "More."

Crane shrugged. "*Ten* . . . thousand?"

"Higher." The excitement in his voice was palpable.

"A hundred thousand."

When Morales shook his head and jerked his thumb towards the ceiling, Crane took another look at the silver-dollar-sized coin sitting in the box.

"Really? More than a hundred? Two?"

"Five!" exclaimed Morales with a laugh. "Five hundred thousand American."

"*Jesus.*" Crane whistled appreciatively and turned to his host. "Half a *million?*"

"Half a million, my friend."

"Shouldn't they be in a museum somewhere? Wouldn't they be safer there?"

"Nah." Morales stroked his mustache down as he took another look at his coins. "They're mine. In fact, no one knows these five exist except for those I allow to see them." He glanced up at Crane, the corners of his eyes crinkling with his teasing smile. "Why? Were you thinking of stealing them?"

Crane barked out a laugh and lifted his hands. "You got me. I confess."

Morales chuckled, then swatted Crane in the chest with the back of his hand in a friendly way. "Come. Enough of these dusty rooms, eh? Let's go see to those drinks. All this talk has made me thirsty."

It was unsettling how easily Crane could see himself being won over by the charismatic Morales, despite the grossly inappropriate fixation on his niece and his apparent interest in Max.

However, all Crane had to do was convince Max the *Federales* knew where they were—*without* revealing that he had almost snitched—and they would skip town before Morales could charm Max into his bed.

You think he hasn't already?

Shut up.

Keeping his smile light, Crane glanced around. The smack to the chest had reminded him he had something to take care of. "Any chance I can use the restroom first?"

"Of course. Right this way."

. . .

Crane peeled the mic off the inside of his shirt, then wound the wire around the little black receiver before wrapping the whole thing up with the fabric tape until it was a small white ball. He glanced out the bathroom window to ensure no one was around, then pushed the screen aside and tossed the incriminating evidence as far as he could.

There. No turning back now.

He buttoned up his shirt and splashed cold water on his face. Meeting his gaze in the mirror, Crane thought he looked calm and collected.

Good.

They would have a drink, wait for Preston to arrive, and hopefully, the nefarious drug deal wouldn't take all afternoon. Then they would go home and start planning where they would go next.

Crane left the bathroom and walked down the long hallway to the stairs.

Australia? Maybe they should go to Australia . . . It was comfortingly remote, *and* he spoke the language. He wouldn't have to rely on Max so much. Then again, wasn't the country rife with poisonous creatures? Maybe England was a better choice.

He looked out over the balustrade. Morales, Espada, Gabriela, and Max were standing around the living room chatting.

"There you are," Max said, spotting him on the gallery. "Come on. I made something special."

Crane took the stairs down and accepted the drink. Whatever was in it was blue, and there was a pink paper umbrella with two cherries anchoring it in the glass. "Uh, thanks."

"Daniel made us wait for you so we can do a toast," Morales said, lifting his drink. "*Conejito*, will you do the honours?"

Max smiled wide, then cleared his throat, holding his glass aloft. "To new friends and new opportunities. And to *Señor* Morales for being a gracious host, inviting us into his beautiful home." He looked over at Crane, and though his smile didn't budge, his gaze grew cold. "To Robert for being such a constant and *loyal* partner."

Crane's heart turned over in his chest, his mouth suddenly dry.

Max knows something.

"I love you, babe," Max said softly. After a moment, he tilted his head, obviously waiting for Crane to reply.

"I love you too," Crane hastily answered. His voice sounded strange in his ears.

Max nodded like he was satisfied, and the warmth returned to his eyes as he gestured to the patio outside with a grin. "And finally, to this gorgeous weather where there's no bloody snow and slush."

Everyone laughed, and Crane joined in with a nervous-sounding titter, his eyes on Max. Maybe he had just imagined it . . .

"*Salud!*"

"*Salud!*" came the resounding chorus.

Crane took a sip of his drink and found it sweet, fruity, and pleasant.

"Do you like it?" Max slid his arm around Crane's waist

and looked up at him with an endearing smile as he put the straw of his cocktail to his lips.

"Yes. I do," Crane replied. He took another few sips to prove to Max that he was speaking the truth. "Thank you."

"Good." Max glanced away, looking in Gabriela's direction.

The young woman was focused on her father and uncle while they debated something in hushed tones.

"What's in this?" Crane asked, drinking more of his cocktail.

"Oh, a bunch of stuff," Max replied vaguely, scrutinizing him again. "Are you feeling all right? You don't look so great."

Just then, a little wave of fatigue washed over Crane. Scrubbing his face with his free hand, he closed his eyes for a moment, then shook his head to rid himself of the strange feeling.

"Yeah. I think so." His stomach gurgled. "I think I just need to eat something."

"Don't worry, we'll sit down soon," Morales said, overhearing him. "Lunch is almost ready on the barbecue."

Crane frowned. "Shouldn't . . . we . . . wait for . . . Preston?" Why was he talking so slowly?

"Who is Preston?" Morales stared at him, his eyes slowly narrowing as Crane's brain seemed to take forever to form an opinion or even a response to the weird question.

"What?" His lips felt weirdly numb.

Max's hand squeezed his waist, and he looked down at the young man. It was like he was standing in a dark tunnel. He rubbed his face again.

"Maybe you should sit down."

"What's . . . goin' on?" He heard a loud thump but couldn't seem to get his neck to turn.

There was . . . no. What had he just . . . hm?

Crane couldn't tell whether he was speaking out loud or not. Why was the carpet on his face?

What . . .

ELEVEN
THE TOOLSHED
PRESENT DAY

FRIDAY, DECEMBER 1ST

Crane groaned and frantically began rocking and shaking, scratching at the leather belt that bound him to the chair. Then he kicked out his legs and twisted his arms as far as they would go, his heart going like a John Bonham solo until his shirt was completely soaked through with sweat. Then, when he realized there was absolutely nothing he could do to escape his predicament, he sagged in the chair, his eyes closed.

After he'd caught his breath, he felt oddly calm.

"All right . . ." he said with a sigh. "Now what?"

"*Wellll.* Now comes the fun part."

Crane heard the chair behind him creak and looked over his shoulder as Max stood up. "How did you get free?"

Max stepped around to face him, a grin on his face. "I was just waiting for you to wake up."

"What happened? The last thing I remember was—" Crane grimaced, desperately sifting through the fog in his head. "I remember you giving . . . that toast." He blinked and looked up at Max. "The drink. Jesus, I think they put something in our drinks."

Max laughed. "No. *I* put something in your drink, silly."

Crane went cold as he stared up at Max for a few very long seconds, the blood singing in his ears. "Max, what . . . did . . . you . . . *do?*" he asked slowly.

"You'll see." Max put his hands on his hips, tilting his head to appraise Crane. "First, we gotta get something out of the way, *don't* we, Doc?"

"Wha—"

"Have you been doing something naughty? Let's see . . ." Max leaned down, reaching for the front of Crane's shirt to unbutton it. "Do we have a surprise in here?"

"You knew about the wire?" Crane whispered, fear stealing his voice. "But wait, I—"

"Of *course*, I knew." Max frowned and paused for a moment after rapidly undoing three buttons. He then slowly undid a fourth and straightened to stare down at Crane with a bemused expression. "Where is it?"

"I threw it out the bathroom window."

"You . . . threw it . . ." A deep crease formed between Max's dark brows.

"Out the window, yeah."

Max's laugh was high and amused, and he slapped his thighs before squatting down in front of Crane. "Oh, *Doc*. You couldn't do it, could you?" He beamed up at him. "You *do* love me."

Crane stared down at Max, starting to feel more annoyed than frightened. "You were *testing* me?"

"And you passed!" Max gave him a cheeky grin. "Huzzah!"

154

Clenching his jaw, Crane took a few steadying breaths. Had Max tipped off the cops himself? Was López in on it? He had a torrent of questions but started with the most crucial: "And . . . had I *failed* your little test? What would you have done?"

"Well. I would have been super sad if you had ratted me out to the po-po." Jutting out his bottom lip in a pout, Max slowly traced his index finger down his cheek in the mimicry of a tear. "But . . . never mind that," Max said dismissively as he rose to his feet again. "We have to get going."

He fished something out of his back pocket and held it up to the light. It was a syringe.

"What's that for?"

"It's for you, dummy. Now, hold still."

"Wait. *No!*" Alarmed, Crane struggled briefly against his bonds as Max pulled the cap off the syringe and pushed the plunger until liquid beaded at the tip of the needle. "Don't do this."

"I said, hold *still.*" Max grunted as he struggled to hold Crane's arm, eventually putting a knee across Crane's thighs to immobilize his arm by holding it at the wrist and leaning his weight into it. "C'mon, Doc, work with me here," he said, exasperated.

Breath coming in gasps, Crane tried to punch or scratch at Max's back, trying to dislodge him, but the belt made it too awkward to do much harm. It took a minute, but Max finally managed to trap his arm palm up. Crane watched in horror as the needle slid easily into his vein with barely a sting.

"What . . . what is it?" Crane swallowed hard. "What are you giving me?"

"Something to make you sleep. A new sedative made by

Farmacéuticos Luján," Max replied, pulling Crane's shirt sleeve over the drop of blood. He pressed his thumb to the fabric, evidently to stop the bleeding. "One that will *hopefully* knock you out for a good long while but won't cause you to go into respiratory arrest. Or flat out kill you."

"Hopefully?" Crane's voice was shrill.

"Don't worry, Doc. Everything is going to be a-okay. Trust me."

Crane's vision was already getting fuzzy, and he felt warm and sleepy as the drug took over. Then, just before he closed his eyes, he heard Max ask him a question.

"Shit. Are you left-handed or right-handed?"

Then Crane was gone.

TWELVE
THE BODY OF EVIDENCE

SATURDAY, DECEMBER 2ND

Crane felt a strange buzzing in his body. The sensation was similar to how he used to feel after a long run, back when he used to do that sort of thing—back when he used to take proper care of himself. He snorted as he turned over sleepily. Who was he kidding? He'd never taken adequate care of himself. The running phase had only happened after Mary called his ass "flat as a pancake."

Pulling the comforter over his shoulder, Crane decided the buzz was more like a rumble and that there was definitely something going on with his left arm. The longer he lay on it, the weirder it felt. It was numb, yet there was a deep distant ache in his forearm and wrist. Crane sighed and turned over again, trying to get comfortable. He kept his eyes shut tight so he wouldn't wake himself further, but it didn't take long to realize it wasn't going to work. He was awake. It was probably time to get up anyway.

Crane opened his eyes, and his first thought was that he had gone blind.

What the hell?

He rolled over onto his back and lifted his head, looking around.

Okay. Not blind.

There was a pale rectangle ahead—the outline of the bedroom door. With a groan, he lay back down on the pillow, wondering what the hell Max was up to. Was this some sort of sensory deprivation experiment? A prank? Maybe it was just really dark out, and Crane had slept the day away. Max had probably drugged him again.

Pondering that idea, Crane realized he felt oddly indifferent. No, not indifferent. Just calm. And . . . rumbling. The rumbling sensation was still there, but it seemed to be coming from outside his body, not from his muscles like previously thought.

Huh.

Reaching to his left, he patted slowly along the bedside table, looking for the lamp. Not only was it not where it usually was, there was also something strange going on when he touched the table. It felt . . . muffled, like there was something between it and his hand. However, when he tried searching with just the tips of his fingers, all he felt was the cool, painted surface. Even weirder than the muffled sensation was that, even as he lay there wondering what on earth was going on, he didn't feel perturbed about any of it. Or anything at all.

It only occurred to him after a few moments of contemplation that the muffled feeling might have something to do with his *hand* and not the table, seeing as it was his left arm he had reached out with, the same one that felt numb and achy.

When Crane discovered his hand was wrapped in rough cloth, a bit of cold anxiety began to crack through his comfortable emotional blankness, so he decided to get out of bed to investigate. The light had to be somewhere.

Crane must have misjudged the distance between the bed and the wall, something he'd only done twice since moving to the condo because he hit his face hard enough to send a jolt of adrenaline through him, which in turn sent up another crackle of anxiety.

Something was definitely amiss.

Feeling dizzy, Crane stumbled around in a darkness that grew increasingly unfamiliar as he searched for the light switch. This was *not* the bedroom in their condo. Worse, he was starting to remember what had happened. The meeting at Morales's house. The toolshed. The syringe.

What the fuck is going on?

He heard quiet whimpers in the dark, and it took him a moment to realize they were coming from him. Panic had fully set in, and he was in real danger of hurting himself if he didn't focus on where he was instead of throwing himself against walls and furniture like a fly trapped in a glass jar. Crane took a few deep breaths to centre himself, then carefully felt along the wall panels.

After a few long minutes of increasingly desperate searching, he found a set of flat buttons around waist height and pressed one. Instantly the dark was replaced with warm light, and Crane stood there, eyes wide, in the entrance to a lavish, oddly familiar bedroom. When he spotted the missing finial on the four-poster bed, he knew why he recognized the room. He was on Preston's yacht.

What the fuck?

With his heart in his throat, Crane looked down. His left hand was swaddled in gauze to the wrist. What had happened to him? He was almost too scared to look. Steeling himself, Crane clenched his jaw as he slowly lifted his hand, staring bug-eyed at what he discovered. The gauze was concentrated in one area, looped over and around his hand, but always passing over the gap where his ring finger should be. Crane swallowed and *very* gently probed the dressing, hoping his finger was bent over, hidden beneath the bandage, but found nothing.

Crane felt sick to his stomach. Clutching his hand to his chest as he panted, he blinked through the black spots in his vision and sat down on the edge of the mattress, closing his eyes. Once he'd gotten his breathing under control, he touched the dressing again, gingerly pressing into it. The pain in his hand was there, but it was distant, and the gauze bandage was clean and skillfully wrapped, meaning someone had taken the time to ensure he was comfortable. However, two things were certain: his finger was *definitely* missing, and, one way or another, Max was to blame.

Anger was slowly breaking through Crane's fear, finally clearing the cobwebs from his mind. He realized the rumbling he had felt earlier was the ship's engine, which meant they were on the move. Crane stood and lifted the blackout curtain from the bedroom window, uncovering a bright oval bisected by two shades of blue—a cloudless sky and waveless sea. It looked like they were no longer in Cancun, where the *Sea La*

Vie had been berthed, but where were they? And, more importantly, where were they going?

Were they on their way to the States with a shipment of drugs? If so, why had Max knocked him out with the spiked drink? Why the amputation? Crane started feeling breathless and dizzy again. He needed answers.

Crane let the curtain drop and walked to the door, wondering if he would find it locked, but the handle turned smoothly at his touch. Opening the door, Crane peered out into the narrow hallway and, finding it empty, took the stairs up to the main deck. He shielded his eyes from the bright sun streaming in through the enormous windows, blinking tears from his eyes as he looked around the empty living area. In the dining room, Crane found a young man polishing a silver tureen.

"Hi. Uh . . . I'm looking for Preston?" Crane asked. When his question was met with a deep, confused frown, he realized he didn't even know Preston's last name. "Vivian?"

"*Si,*" the crewmember said, brightening. He pointed towards the big patio doors.

"Thank you. *Gracias.*"

Crane went outside and didn't see anyone at first, but on hearing a giggle, he went around the hot tub and past the big shaded sitting area, where he found Vivian and Gabriela lounging topless on deck chairs. As Crane approached, still clutching his wounded hand to his chest, Gabriela lifted a joint to her lips and took a deep drag.

"*Hola, papi,*" she said, then exhaled a giant cloud of skunky pot smoke, grinning up at him, her green-eyed gaze soft and hazy.

"Rob! How you feelin', honey?" Vivian asked, giving him

a sympathetic smile. She lifted her sunglasses to look up at him, her blue eyes crinkling at the corners. "You okay?"

Crane didn't know how to answer, given that he didn't know what the fuck was going on.

"I've been better. Where's Max?" Ironically, he was asking for the one person *guaranteed* not to give him a straight answer.

"You shouldn't be out of bed."

Startled, he turned around and found Max in the nude with a drink in each hand. The young man wrinkled his brow at Crane in disapproval before skirting around him to deliver the drinks to the women. His bikini tan lines had faded, but as he bent over, Crane saw he still had a barely visible inverted triangle just above his ass crack.

"There you go, ladies. Néstor made them strong, so pace yourselves. And you"—Max took Crane by the bicep, wrapping his other arm around his lower back to turn him back towards the patio doors—"need to take it easy."

Crane started to resist but discovered he was feeling dizzy again now that his adrenaline was running out, so he let Max steer him into the yacht's interior. They ran into two crewmembers in the hallway chatting as they carried armfuls of folded linen. They stopped and gave Crane and Max a cheerful greeting, completely unfazed by Max's nudity, and Crane realized the whole vibe aboard the ship differed from last time. Everyone seemed more at ease.

Crane grunted as he was deposited gently by Max onto a big comfortable sofa in the ship's main salon.

"What the *hell* happened, Max?" He clenched his jaw, staring up at the naked young man. "What's going on?"

Max smiled and leaned down to cup his cheek affectionately. "I'll show you. But first, how are you feeling? Not too much pain?"

"No. Not much," Crane replied, though his hand was starting to throb. "Why am I missing a finger?" He kept his voice calm even though just saying the words made him feel ill.

"Because I cut it off." Max laughed at Crane's expression before throwing himself onto the couch next to him. He looked over and twisted his face into a mock scowl, evidently mirroring the expression Crane wore, then quickly pecked a kiss on Crane's lips before he could stop him. "Relax. You're going to thank me."

"I very much doubt that," Crane replied through clenched teeth.

"Watch." Max used a remote to turn the closest TV on, then fiddled with a complicated looking remote for a few seconds before an image of a familiar Canadian news anchor appeared on the big flatscreen.

After a second, the video started playing.

. . . and in other news, the body of Dr. Dennis Crane, the Montréal-based psychologist convicted of several shocking crimes, including the murder of his next-door neighbour and the kidnap and torture of one of his patients, was found Friday evening in Tulum, Mexico.

Dr. Crane, who escaped prison custody in May of this year, disappeared without a trace in the Laurentians, baffling law officials and leading them to believe that at least one high-

profile crime syndicate was involved in facilitating his getaway.

The discovery of Dr. Crane's body in Mexico came only weeks after local Mexican authorities intercepted security footage on the dark web showing the Smith's Falls, Ontario, native apparently being held captive and in distress in an unknown location. Officials attempted to trace the source of the footage but were unable to extract any usable data from the—

"Wait!" Crane leaned forward, alarmed. "I've *seen* that video."

Max paused the video and turned to Crane, his brows high. "Oh, yeah?"

On the screen was the grainy black-and-white image of the screaming man in the chair. The reflection of the restaurant's neon lights on the surface of the television, as well as the distance and size of the small set, had made it impossible to recognize himself the day he had first seen it, but now, up on the big flatscreen, it was obvious.

"I don't understand w—"

"Shhh. Pay attention." Max patted Crane's knee and hit play on the remote.

. . . later made the grisly discovery of Dr. Crane's remains at the residence of a prominent Mexican businessman, Jorge Morales, owner and CEO of Farmacéuticos Luján, a fast-growing local pharmaceutical company.

Firefighters were called to Morales's home on Friday

evening after neighbours reported seeing thick plumes of smoke coming from Mr. Morales's property. When officials arrived on the scene, Morales and his brother Carlos Espada, COO of Farmacéuticos Luján, were discovered outside on the patio, unconscious. The two men were quickly revived by paramedics and treated for smoke inhalation.

The source of the smoke was traced to a fire in a small shed at the rear of the townhouse. Officials believe the fire may have started from a combination of improperly stored gasoline, compost, and gardening chemicals but have not yet released their final report.

Once firefighters were able to get the blaze under control, they entered the shed to discover human remains within.

The following details may be disturbing to some. Viewers, please be advised.

Crane blinked at the video of two men carrying a body bag between them and turned to Max. He was watching him with an excited gleam in his eye. Discomfited, Crane turned back to the recorded news segment.

. . . DNA evidence was destroyed by the fire. However, the coroner on the scene estimated that the remains belonged to a male between the ages of forty and sixty, possibly Caucasian, and approximately one hundred and ninety centimetres, or six foot three in height. The body was found bound to a metal chair, apparently the victim of lengthy torture—the man's teeth and jaw had been shattered with a blunt object, and several of his fingers removed.

The mystery man's identity was finally determined early Saturday morning with the discovery of a severed finger and a pair of blood-covered garden shears in one of the upstairs rooms at the Morales residence. Fingerprinting revealed that the severed digit belonged to none other than Canadian fugitive, Dr. Dennis Crane.

From there, investigators could positively match the background of the dark web video to Jorge Morales's home, in particular a painting by famed local artist María Natalia Robles. And finally, footage taken from Morales's security system was found showing Dr. Crane in restraints in the backyard shed, the timestamp coinciding with Friday's fire.

Officials have not yet determined the link between Dr. Dennis Crane and Jorge Morales. More to come.

Now . . . Are you looking for this holiday season's perf—

The video stopped, and Crane sat there, his head spinning.

"I don't understand," he whispered. "I saw that video of me in the chair . . . like, two *weeks* ago." He stopped and frowned. "And you told me I had hallucinated it."

Shrugging, Max smiled. "Maybe you didn't."

"But how is it possible? Friday was the first time I ever went to Morales's house." Something occurred to him. "Rewind. Show me the video again."

Max chuckled. "You betcha, boss."

Once more, the grainy video was on screen, Crane's face distorted in a crazed scream. Behind him was the painting of *Xolotl* hanging on the wall, just like it was hanging at Morales's . . . *and* at the condo. Crane scrutinized the floor beneath the chair in the video.

"This was taken in our living room."

"How do you figure that?"

"There's no rug. Morales has this huge Turkish rug in that room."

"Look at you, Mister Smarty Pants."

Crane shook his head, staring at the television. "It was the day you drugged me the second time, wasn't it? Those are the clothes I was wearing. And that's why I look so insane. *And* why I can't remember any of it."

"Yep. I had to pay the downstairs neighbours a wad of dough to keep them from calling the cops. You were screaming your head off." Max stretched his arms up with a yawn, then scratched the centre of his chest, where the hair was starting to grow back in sparse patches. Then he leaned his head on Crane's shoulder, tucking an arm around Crane's waist.

"So, I'm *dead?*" Cold horror had slowly seeped into his veins over the course of the video, and he sat there, numb and confused.

"Dead, dead, deadski." Max snuggled closer, pushing the tip of his nose into the side of Crane's neck. "No one is going to look for you anymore. Right at this moment, our friend Mr. Espada is at a press conference telling everyone that his dear big brother lent a sum of money to a Mr. Montagnet back in July and that the naughty Mr. Montagnet failed to pay him back in a timely fashion. This made Mr. Morales *very* mad, prompting him to take matters into his own hands, which is totally believable when one has a history of causing bodily harm to not one, not two, but *three* individuals."

"Oh?" Crane's voice sounded far away. There was

something about the news segment that was gnawing at him . . . Something he was missing. Something out of place.

"Yeah. He greased a few palms to make those go away. This time, it's in the international spotlight. He's going away for sure."

"Won't he deny everything?"

"*You* denied everything. Look where that got you."

Crane gave a hollow laugh. "You set him up, just like you set me up."

"Hey, it's for the best, love."

"But *why*?"

Scowling, Max curled his lip. "I just don't like the fucking guy."

"So, is that why you framed *me*?" Crane asked in a quiet voice and was surprised by the immediate change in Max's expression. He looked shocked and appalled.

"No! Nuh-uh. Not at all. No way." Max shook his head. "That was different."

"Right."

"Gee willikers, Doc, I swear. Cross my heart. Don't you believe me?"

Crane changed the subject so he didn't have to answer that. "So, Morales really *isn't* the head of some cartel?"

"Nope. That was just to make it super fun and exciting for you. Luján's just a big pharmaceutical company. But a shady-as-hell one. They found out the cholesterol drugs they were developing had some *pretty* interesting side effects and—"

"Oh my god." Crane blinked. "That *víbora* drug?"

"Yep. And its sibling—*la araña*. Though . . . I'm the one who came up with those names. They're actually called something totally unpronounceable." A grin flashed across Max's face before he sobered again. "Morales was drawing up contracts to sell them to a few *very* interested parties."

"Who?"

"Ones with huge *military* budgets."

"Oh." Crane rubbed a hand over his mouth. "I see." Which was better? The drugs in the hands of a terrorist group or a military power? He swallowed, his throat suddenly dry. "Jesus Christ."

Max chuckled. "I knew you'd say that."

"So, what happens now that Morales is going to jail?"

"Ownership of Luján passes on to his brother Carlos."

"But, won't Carlos do the same as his brother? With the contracts?"

"Meh. No idea. But I do like him loads better. He's a snappy dresser, and his daughter is a fucking hoot." Max's eyes narrowed slowly as Crane sat there in silence. Then, after a moment, he asked, "Aren't you happy? You're a free man now."

Crane stared at Max. *Free from the law, but not really free, am I? And at what cost? A finger? And something . . . else . . .* What was he missing?

The screensaver on the TV came to life then, treating them to a slow slideshow of naked, big-breasted women on jet skis. Something told Crane Preston had curated the collection himself.

Preston.

Heart pounding, Crane blinked rapidly at the screen, seeing nothing. "Max, whose body was burned in the shed?" he asked, dread making his voice tight. Why was he bothering to ask when he already knew the answer?

"Oh, don't you worry yourself about that." Max gave a little laugh, taking up Crane's injured hand in his to kiss the gauze. He squeezed it none too gently, making Crane wince. "How about we get you something to help with the pain, eh, my darling?" And with a pointed look, Max put an end to Crane's questions.

"Yes," Crane said faintly, closing his eyes. "Thank you."

THIRTEEN
THE BEGINNING OF THE END

SUNDAY, DECEMBER 3RD

Crane sat there pushing the peas around his plate, too dazed to lift any food to his mouth. Latin dance music blared from the yacht's speakers, drowning out the giggling conversation between Vivian and Max. He lifted his eyes, the strings of colourful lights making streaks in his vision, and focused on Gabriela, dancing nearby with two men in crew uniforms. The young woman wore a sheer camisole dress with nothing on underneath—she might as well have been naked.

"Doc? You want more wine?" Max asked, slinging an arm around his shoulders. He kissed Crane on the temple and, not waiting for him to reply, refilled his glass nearly to the brim.

Taking a sip of the outrageously expensive wine, Crane closed his eyes. Between the painkillers, the antibiotics, and the alcohol, he was feeling no pain. In fact, he wasn't feeling anything at all, and he was absolutely fine with that. He sighed and glanced up again, catching Vivian's eye, and the woman smiled flirtatiously at him over her glass. Pretending he hadn't noticed, Crane looked out over the railing at the deep blackness that hugged the ship like a velvet cloak. Below, the sea glimmered with tiny reflections of the brightly lit yacht slicing her inky waters like a shining knife.

They were en route to Sint Maarten, a trip that would have taken roughly two days at the yacht's top speed, but since their flight to Madrid was only on the evening of the sixth, they'd decided to take their time. Max, Vivian, and Gabriela, that was. Crane hadn't been consulted.

The peas did another complete circuit before the serving crewmember reached down to take his plate away.

"Let me, *señor*." The young man smiled at Crane, his smile white against his dark skin.

Another crewmember set a new plate in front of him—this time, it was fish and rice. Crane sighed, looking away from the dish. He had no appetite. Turning his attention back to the dancers, he watched the two men grind against Gabriela, front and back. The young woman had her head thrown back, sweat shimmering on her brow, lost in the moment.

In front of him, Vivian was staring ahead of her, her eyes distant and a little wrinkle marring her smooth, freckled brow. He'd seen that faraway look more and more over the last two days—cracks were beginning to appear. Noticing his attention, the "grieving" widow gave him a wide, friendly smile that took a second too long to reach her eyes.

Crane's pulse thudded dully in his ears, out of sync with the pounding rhythm of the dance music as his thoughts struggled weakly through the poisoned miasma that had invaded his brain. With a grimace, he reached for the bottle of wine with his good hand.

His *good* hand. He'd never have two good hands again.

The bottle tipped, and Crane lost his grip, the wine spreading like a bloodstain across the white tablecloth.

"Ruh-roh," Max said, standing quickly to save the wine bottle before it fell to the deck. "That's okay, Doc. We'll go get another."

"No." Crane rubbed his face as he got to his feet a little unsteadily. "I'm . . . tired. I'm going to bed."

"You sure? Party's just getting started."

"Yeah." He swallowed thickly, feeling a little nauseous as he braced himself against the railing.

"Want me to come with you? I'll tuck you in . . ."

"No. I'm fine." Crane tugged on the hem of his shirt and smoothed the front down with his bandaged hand to tidy it. "Stay. Have fun. I'll see you later."

"You sure will, mister." Max gave him a cheeky grin.

Crane wondered if he'd wake up with his dick in Max's mouth like the previous night. They'd fucked until dawn—murder, deception, and mayhem clearly did nothing to quash his appetite for the young man. He was beginning to wonder if anything ever would.

He carefully made his way down the exterior steps, and as he moved further away from the glaring lights of the upper deck, stars began to appear above him. Standing at the rear of the yacht, Crane gazed up in awe at the watercolour brushstrokes of the bright Milky Way seeping into the deep sparkling indigo of the night sky.

For a few terribly brief moments, Crane was at peace.

A high-pitched giggle split the air, followed by a sudden jump in the music's volume, and Crane sighed. Sleep couldn't come soon enough.

Entering the main deck through the patio doors, Crane

crossed the dining room and the salon and decided to stop at the bar to grab a nightcap. As he picked through the bottles, he glanced at the newspaper clipping someone had taped to the wall next to the shelves. It was too dark to read it, but he knew what it said almost by heart.

MILLIONAIRE MISSING, PRESUMED DEAD

Preston Ashburnum, 42, son of American oil magnate Chick Ashburnum, disappeared on Thursday, Nov. 30, while on a solo night dive off the coast of Cancun, Mexico. Though a seasoned diver, Ashburnum was known for taking unnecessary risks and may have ignored repeated warnings of a heavy undertow. He disappeared at approximately 9:30 p.m. on Thursday and was reported missing an hour later by his ship's crew when he hadn't yet surfaced.

Officials believe he may have been injured or suffered an equipment failure and was pulled out to sea, subsequently drowning. A similar drowning occurred in the area in August 2012.

Though Ashburnum's body has yet to be recovered, no foul play is suspected at this time.

He is survived by his wife of three years, Vivian Plemonds . . .

"No foul play." Crane quietly repeated the words to himself as he decided on the bottle of Japanese whisky. After cracking the seal, he poured a generous amount into a cut crystal glass and stood in the gloom staring at the barely visible picture of the "happy" couple accompanying the news article. Brow furrowed, Crane took a sip of the whisky Preston hadn't lived long enough to try.

Wasn't the world a better place without the likes of Preston Ashburnum? Maybe.

That's the spirit, Doc. Now you're getting it.

"Doc?"

Heart racing, Crane turned around.

"I thought you were going to bed." Max took a step towards him.

He was bare-chested, and strands of his dark hair stuck to his forehead. The sweat on his body caught the deck lighting outside the salon windows making his torso faintly glisten as he breathed. Crane guessed he'd been dancing.

"I am," Crane replied at length after trying the whisky again. It was really good.

Cheers, you dickhead, he said silently to Preston's ghost.

Biting his bottom lip, Max came a little closer, his eyes unreadable in the near dark. "Do you want company?" he asked, his voice husky.

Crane stared at him for a few heartbeats, then downed the rest of the whisky in one swallow. Finally, he grabbed the bottle and turned to go, then looked back at Max after a few steps—the road to hell was paved with good whiskey and a doting psychopath with a voracious appetite for cock.

"Well? Are you coming or what?"

Max grinned.

○

WEDNESDAY, DECEMBER 6TH

Crane flipped through the clothes in Preston's closet again, choosing two pairs of light-coloured chinos, khaki and tan, and the only three long-sleeved button-downs he could find. The weather in Madrid hovered around 10°C this time of year, and most of Preston's clothing on board the *Sea La Vie* was beach or cruisewear. *Not* ideal.

Then there was the matter of shoes. Crane looked down at his scuffed canvas sneakers. The one on the right was all right, if a bit dingy, but there was a noticeable bloodstain on the left one, presumably from when Max relieved him of his finger. There was nothing he could do about it, in any case. While he and Preston were roughly the same height, the same couldn't be said for the size of their feet—contrary to the theory about shoe size and dick length, Preston's shoes were too small for Crane.

He closed the closet door and scrutinized himself in the full-length mirror. He had shaved, and Vivian had given him a trim, so he looked pretty decent. And, dressed in Preston's pricey duds, he seemed downright respectable—maybe no one would notice his feet. Crane sighed.

He grabbed a few pairs of boxers and socks, then after a thought, he opened the top drawer next to the mirrored closet where he had seen a glass-topped case full of expensive watches.

"You don't mind, do you, old buddy?" Crane told Preston's ghost as he chose a gunmetal watch out of the case, strapping it on just below the gauze on his wrist. "Course not. What's mine is yours, and yours is mine and all that."

He grimaced, pushing the image of Max and Preston out of his mind. Hallucination or not, he wished he could erase it from his memories.

He quickly stuffed the clothes into the dark-blue day pack he'd found among Preston's belongings and headed for the front of the yacht. The only thing left to pack was the white shirt he'd worn to Morales's house—the ship's laundry staff had promised him they could get the blood out in time for their departure.

Crane took the stairs down to the tank deck, the area of the ship that housed the laundry facilities and kitchen, as well as the crew quarters, and knocked on the door to the laundry room.

A woman poked her head out. *"Si?"*

When she saw Crane, she smiled and gestured for him to enter. There were three stacks of laundry machines at the far end of the room, shelves full of sheets and towels along one wall and a long table, presumably for folding clothing, pushed up against the other. Near the door was a small round table with four chairs, and it was here that the two laundresses were seated, along with the young man responsible for serving breakfast and dinner and the heavy-set maid he had met the first time aboard the *Sea La Vie*. On the table, a small television hooked up to the yacht's satellite TV system was playing a Spanish-language show.

"I'm here for my—" He stopped when all eyes turned towards him in non-so-subtle annoyance. "Shirt," he ended quietly as everyone returned to the on-screen drama.

The woman who had opened the door, one of the mechanical staff, judging by her grey jumpsuit, leaned towards him. "Telenovelas are a very serious thing," she whispered. "It's best to wait for a commercial break."

"Gotcha." He gave her a faint smile, and she winked back at him.

Crane crossed his arms and waited, watching the tiny figures on the TV set argue in rapid Spanish. Mary used to watch a soap opera, but he couldn't think of the name. Something about days or worlds or . . . lives? She'd had to stop because of the extra nursing shifts she took to cover expenses while he was finishing his PhD. Crane remembered how annoyed she'd been about missing the reveal about who had fathered some baby on the show.

The smile dropped from his face as he blinked the memory away. It did no good to remind himself of those days. They might as well have happened to someone else.

As he stood there in silence, wondering how American soap operas compared to Latin American telenovelas or the equivalent in Québec—the *téléroman*—a new character appeared on the screen that looked oddly familiar.

Squinting, Crane leaned forward, a funny, anxious feeling in the pit of his stomach as he watched the man speak sternly to the two women on set. When the man pulled a stethoscope out of a bag, Crane knew where he'd seen him before.

He swallowed, his pulse throbbing in his temples as he watched the doctor tilt his head from side to side as he contemplated something before giving an explanation to his patient . . . just as he had when Crane had asked him whether the swelling in his brain was serious. Crane balled his fists, letting out a gasp when the left hand sent a shooting pain up his arm, then he breathed out slowly through his nose and cleared his throat lest his voice fail him.

"Is that man a doctor in real life?" he murmured to the woman next to him.

"What?" She turned to him with a quiet laugh, looking at him like he was crazy. "No. That's Ciro Domínguez. He's an actor. Isn't he handsome?"

"Jesus *fucking* Christ."

The woman jerked back in shock, her dark eyes wide, and Crane apologized, excusing himself. Abandoning his stained shirt, he left for the stairs and took two steps at a time up to the sun deck where he knew Max was working. He burst through the doors, startling the young man, and stood there glowering at him while he caught his breath.

"Woah. What's up with you?" Max's brows pinched together above his nose as he stared up at Crane.

"I was never sick . . . *was I?*"

Max looked confused.

"I just saw *Doctor* Aguilar on TV."

"Oh." Max chuckled. "*That.* Yeah, no. I mean, the tummy troubles were real, but th—"

Crane stepped forward, looming over Max. "All the fucking things I hallucinated . . . it was all real, wasn't it? You just lied and gaslit and bullshitted, and you fucking—" He grimaced, panting out a few quick, furious breaths. "Oh god, you fucking *sucked Preston's fucking cock*, you little shit, right in front of me, and you . . . *argh!*" Crane hunched over, literally quaking with anger. He grabbed the sides of his head, feeling as if his fury would blow his skull apart, and clenched his teeth against the pain in his mangled hand.

"Uhh . . ." For a long moment, Max just stared up at him. The subtle amusement in his expression just made Crane angrier.

"You lie and you lie and you lie," Crane said in a barely restrained voice. "And I keep taking it and taking it like a fucking idiot."

"You're not a fucking idio—"

"Shut up." He snatched a handful of Max's hair and pulled his head back hard enough that Max let out a small whimper, though he made no attempt to free himself. "I just . . ." Crane swallowed and looked up, trying to get the tempest raging through him under control long enough to get answers. "How did you make me think I killed your mother?" He met Max's gaze again. "That's the only one I can't figure out. Was it really your mother? Was she in on it? Was it makeup? How did you clean so fast?"

Blinking rapidly, Max swallowed, keeping his dark eyes on him. "It never happened, Doc."

"*Bullshit.*" Crane shook Max, eliciting another quiet cry of pain.

"It was the drug. *La araña.* Y-you came back with the food, and I dosed your *aguas frescas.* I wanted to see for myself what it could do. I just told you what I wanted you to see . . . and you saw it. I swear."

Drawing back, Crane studied Max's expression, then loosened his grip on his hair a touch, though not enough to let him escape. The explanation sounded plausible—how else would Crane's hands have been covered in blood one minute and clean the next? Flaring his nostrils, Crane ground his back teeth together, feeling the muscles in his jaw flex as he contemplated Max.

"You sucked Preston's cock," he said quietly. "That really happened?"

Max averted his eyes, focusing on Crane's wrist, and let out a low whistle of appreciation. "Hey, that's a super nice watch," he said, blatantly changing the subject to avoid answering. "That's gotta be worth . . . fifteen grand?"

Crane clenched his fist in Max's hair, causing him to yelp, then gave him a few violent shakes.

"Okay! Okay! Quit it." He took a deep breath. "Yes. I

sucked Preston's cock. What of it?" Max wrinkled his brow up but didn't add anything.

"Did you do it to make me angry?"

"No," Max replied. He tried to move his head, but Crane held him fast. "It was just . . . the right thing to do at the time." Max cleared his throat. "Hey, what's worse? Him beating on Viv, or me giving him head?"

"Don't do that." Crane gave Max another firm shake, but his anger was already fading, replaced by his habitual lassitude. "Don't *fucking* make excuses." He released Max and sat down across from him, exhausted.

Max rubbed the back of his head, wincing as he watched Crane warily. "I'm sorry."

"No, you're not." Crane sighed and looked away over the clear blue water. "And Inspector López? Who is he, really?"

"Dave's a night janitor at the Mayakoba. He's an aspiring actor."

"Of *course* he is." Crane shook his head.

"So, he was believable, eh? I'll give Domínguez's agent a call. He owes me." Max drummed his fingers on the fibreglass tabletop. "Doc?" he said. "Dennis? Look at me."

Crane scrubbed at his face with his good hand, keeping his eyes averted for a moment longer before relenting. Max had a strange expression on his face. If Crane didn't know any better, he would have thought the young man looked embarrassed. "What?"

"I'm sorry I made you think you were sick for so long."

"Right."

"No, I want to tell you something."

"Okay?"

Shoulders oddly high, Max glanced down at the table for

a few breaths before meeting Crane's eye again. "I didn't just do it to learn about the drug. That was part of it. But, also, I realized I, uh . . . like taking care of you."

Crane couldn't help the laugh that burst out of him like a hiccup.

"No, really," Max said, giving him a look of reproach. "I'm serious. I like how you are when you're like that."

"What? Drugged? Poisoned?"

"I like it when you *need* me. You act different. You're *nicer* to me."

"Yeah, I'm terrified that if I'm not, you'll just leave me to fend for myself," Crane said with a wry grin, somewhat discomfited by Max's earnest tone. "It's called self-preservation."

"Doc, I'm being serious."

"*Max*," Crane replied, mimicking his sober expression, "so am I."

Max rolled his eyes and looked away, his fingers once more beating out a rapid tattoo on the white fibreglass.

Watching Max for a moment, Crane sat back in his chair. "Okay, so you like it when I'm incapacitated because I need you and treat you nicely when I am." He chuckled. "That sounds awfully—"

"—codependent." Max glanced his way again briefly, still looking oddly flustered. "Yeah, I'm well aware."

"Darling . . ."

Max turned to him, eyes wide at Crane's remarkable use of the word.

"I might be a shitty psychologist, but even I could have told you that this"—he motioned to the space between the two of them—"has been codependent from the get-go."

Max lifted his eyebrows but didn't reply. Instead, he gave Crane a very shallow nod.

Crane had called Max "darling" in jest, but it hadn't felt exactly *wrong* to call him that. Reaching out, he stilled Max's fidgeting hands by covering them with his own.

"You know . . ." he said, smiling. "You don't have to drug me or make me think that I'm sick for me to be nice to you. In fact, if you did *less* of that, I might be *more* inclined to be nice to you."

"Yeah." Max chuckled, then shrugged. "Maybe you have a point."

"I know I do." Crane held Max's hands for a moment longer, then sat back again, knowing full well that it was ludicrous to hope this was some miraculous breakthrough. Max was simply manipulating Crane into sympathizing with him for how he'd been treated. It was pure insanity. Codependent, indeed.

"So," he asked, keeping his tone light. "Why are we going to Madrid?"

Max's face creased into a slow grin. "It's a surprise."

FOURTEEN
THE HAPPILY EVER AFTER

WEDNESDAY, DECEMBER 6TH

After parting ways with Vivian in Sint Maarten, Crane, Max, and Gabriela took a shuttle to the airport to catch their flight. The wealthy heiress had sent them off with a cheerful, slightly teary farewell.

Crane couldn't help but notice that it was a little *too* ebullient, even for the ordinarily perky Vivian. As the small van took the windy road to the Princess Juliana International Airport, Crane thought about the bleakness he could see lurking behind Vivian's cheerful veneer and wondered again what part she had personally played in Preston's "disappearance." However, as with the late Mr. Bertrand, Crane thought it was better to stay in the dark about such things.

Coward.

Crane couldn't argue with that assessment.

. . .

At the airport, Max had Crane and Gabriela wait while he went to the Transfer Information Desk to retrieve something. On his return, he handed Crane a Canadian passport.

Mystified, Crane opened it, surprised to see it bore his picture and a new name.

"Chuck Noland?" he said, glancing up at Max. It sounded vaguely familiar. He looked back at the passport. "Chuck? *Really?* And I'm from Winnipeg?"

"Pleased to meet you, Chuck," Max replied with a grin, then held out his hand for Crane's other forged passport. "And so long, Robert and Dan." he threw the two passports they'd arrived with into the nearest trash can.

"But, I don't know anything about Winnipeg." Crane scrutinized the passport, flipping through the stiff pages. In it were stamps from France, Germany, and Denmark.

Max shrugged. "You can read the Wikipedia page while we wait for our flight."

"But why am I the only one with a new passport and new name?" Crane asked. "What about you and Gabi?"

"Well, Gabi's not linked to a murder, and neither is Édouard Duvernay," Max replied. "Dennis Crane, aka Robert Montagnet, might be deceased, but it's best to be prudent, what hey?"

"*Claro,*" Gabriela said, then looked up from her phone, her green eyes wide. "Who is Édouard Duvernay?"

"I'll explain later, *querida.*" Max's cheeks dimpled. "But, right now we need to go buy some plane tickets."

Crane frowned. "But I went through passport check at the port here," he said. "They have my info."

"*Do* they?" Max asked, his eyebrows high. "Are you *certain?*"

Crane opened his mouth to reply in the affirmative, then closed it, his brow furrowed. The woman at the desk had taken his passport and looked at it, but he couldn't remember seeing her enter the information anywhere. The place had been jam-packed with cruise ship passengers, and the workers had all looked harried and impatient for their shifts to end.

"Is that why we didn't go to the bay closest to the airport? More people, less security?"

Max touched the side of his nose. "Bingo." Then he held his hand out to Crane.

Crane stared at it for a few seconds, his mouth set in a hard line.

"Oh c'mon, Doc. It's not like we're fucking in public. I just want to hold your hand." Max wiggled his fingers. "What's a little hand-holding between pals?"

Gabriela giggled and shook her head, going back to her phone.

With a sigh, Crane relented and took Max's hand. Apart from a few stares, no one seemed to care what they were doing, and he had to admit to himself that it was actually nice walking hand-in-hand with Max. Lifting his chin, Crane levelled a challenging look at a middle-aged man who met his eye across the corridor, but all he got in return was a wistful smile.

The flight from Sint Maarten to New York was uneventful. Crane stayed conscious long enough to wash down a painkiller with a Jack and Coke, only waking up when the plane's landing gear hit the runway.

At JFK, they had to make a mad dash to catch their

connecting flights because of a delay with Gabriela's baggage, followed by a lengthy wait at US Customs, but once they were on the plane, Crane started to relax. Everything was going as planned, as far as he knew.

They were flying Lufthansa for the trip's final leg, and the business class seats were comfortable and roomy compared to their earlier flight. Gabriela was a row ahead of them, seated next to a man who immediately tried to get the pretty young woman to chat with him.

Crane watched as she snapped her gum loudly a few times, glaring at the man with such a jaundiced eye that Crane had to cough to cover his laugh. She then *very* deliberately placed her bright-purple headphones over her ears while the man continued speaking, only turning away when he finally got the hint.

Amused, Crane looked over at Max, only to find him snoozing in his seat. Once they had taken off, the flight attendant showed Crane the button to convert the seat into a narrow bed, and he slowly moved Max into a fully reclined position while she pulled out a blanket and pillow for him to use.

Having already slept for hours, Crane wasn't tired and eventually was pulled into a conversation with the young couple across the aisle. The women were students at the Universidad Autónoma de Madrid, one in environmental science and the other in psychology, and were coming back from an all-expenses paid trip they had won on the internet. The three of them spoke in hushed voices in the darkened cabin, but eventually, they too wanted to get some sleep, leaving Crane alone with his thoughts.

Bored, he rifled through the magazines and newspapers

tucked into the seat pocket in front of him, then turned on the little reading light built into his seat. Unfortunately, his glasses had been lost somewhere between Morales's house and the *Sea La Vie*. *Still, even* if he could see without squinting, nothing in the selection of reading materials was interesting enough to distract him.

His brain kept ping-ponging from Morales, who undoubtedly would swear up and down to everyone that Crane was still alive, to Preston's death and the guilt Vivian had inherited along with her riches, to the fake doctor and federal agent . . . then his hand would throb and he'd find himself back in that humid toolshed, afraid for his life, only for his mind to quickly turn back to Morales and begin the cycle anew.

Crane rubbed his temples, wishing he could shut his brain down, and ordered another whiskey sour when the flight attendant passed by on her rounds a few minutes later.

"Are you all right?" she asked in a soft German accent as she handed him his glass. "You look a little pale."

"I'll be fine." He smiled and thanked her, though he frowned as she walked away.

He *was* feeling . . . off. Then, wondering if he was coming down with something again, he let out a tiny rueful laugh. Max would be happy if he were getting sick, wouldn't he? Crane looked over at his sleeping companion. It *was* nice being taken care of by the young man. He was certainly more attentive than Mary had ever been—though his ex-wife was a nurse, her bedside manner left much to be desired.

Staring at Max, Crane's brow furrowed as something occurred to him. Max had been extremely attentive, yes, but was that because he genuinely enjoyed taking care of him, or was there an ulterior motive? By keeping Crane abed and occupied, Max had conveniently prevented him from accessing any news . . . news which undoubtedly would have been covering theories about Crane's whereabouts following the release of that disturbing black-and-white video of him.

Chewing on the inside of his cheek, Crane sat back in his seat, staring ahead without seeing anything. He knew which explanation he *wanted* to believe, but was it the truth? And why had Max kept him in the dark about the plan with Morales to begin with? Had he done it to keep Crane from worrying? Or was it so Crane wouldn't have a chance to veto his plan to maim him?

Surely, there were better ways to fake his death? Staring at his hand, Crane flexed it slowly a few times and winced. One thing was for sure—he'd never be able to wear a wedding ring on that finger again. Crane blinked, then looked over at Max.

Maybe that was the point?

After a moment, Crane smirked, shaking his head over his late-night reveries and pressed the button to summon the flight attendant—he needed another drink.

THURSDAY, DECEMBER 7TH

Bleary-eyed, Crane stared at the red plastic egg in Max's hand. Larger than the toy-filled plastic eggs he'd seen in vending machines at the mall, it made him think of popular commercials from the early nineties. The ads had been about pantyhose that came in egg-shaped plastic containers similar in size to the one Gabriela had handed to Max.

"What is it?" Crane asked, confused.

Max grinned and twisted the egg until the top popped off.

Crane instantly recognized the contents. "Jesus." He glanced around to see if anyone was watching as Max poured over half a million dollars' worth of Spanish doubloons into his palm. The coins were bigger and heavier than they had looked in the glass case. Clenching his jaw, he stared hard at Max.

"So, framing Morales didn't actually have anything to do with getting the cops off my trail? This was all about *money*?"

Max just gave a little shrug and grinned. "Two birds . . ." He laughed at Crane's glower. "I have a buyer here in Madrid that will give us nearly full value. Baby, we'll be set for a good long while with the proceeds, *and* the cops are no longer looking for you. I call that a win-win."

Crane shook his head as he turned the *Tricentenario Real* over to see the other side, too zonked by alcohol and lack of sleep to beleaguer the point any further. What was the point anyway? Max was probably right.

"Ooh? What's this?"

Crane looked up as Max pulled a tiny black velvet pouch from the bottom half of the plastic egg.

"A little extra something," Gabriela replied, biting the corner of her lip as she watched Max tip a dozen or so sparkling jewels into his hand.

Max squinted as he pushed the colourful gemstones around his cupped palm with an index finger. "What? No diamonds? You have a cigar tube full of them and couldn't part with a single one?"

"Pff." Gabriela grinned, her expression playful. "I'm the one who smuggled them out, so I'm the one who decides who gets to keep them, *flaco*."

Frowning at the young woman, Crane asked, "How *did* you get everything past security?"

"Honest, I could have just walked with them in my purse, but I dunno. Better to be safe . . . And they were tucked away somewhere *very* safe." Gabriela's eyes crinkled at the corners as she smiled up at him. "It's a surprise I didn't sound like a *maraca* when I walked."

"Oh?" Crane said, curious. Then he looked at the egg again and suddenly remembered what Max and Gabriela had been up to when he found them together in the condo. The plastic egg was just a little smaller than Max's fist. "*Oh.*" He could also make an educated guess about where the cigar tube had been stashed.

Gabriela let out a peal of laughter at Crane's expression and said something in Spanish to Max, who nodded and laughed in return.

Red-faced, Crane averted his eyes, annoyed that his discomfort amused them so much, and pinched the bridge of his nose, his headache made worse by their mockery. He wondered if they also made fun of him while they undoubtedly fucked on the sly.

"Okay, I need my bag," Gabriela said, pocketing her phone. She jerked her head in the direction of baggage claim. "*Vamos.*"

. . .

The crowd in front of the carousel was densely packed, so Max went ahead to watch for the suitcase while Gabriela and Crane hung back.

"Hey, what's with that sour-lemon face?" Gabriela asked after a few minutes of silence had passed.

Crane sighed and rubbed his hand over his forehead, hating that people could so easily see it when something was on his mind.

"It's nothing. I just . . ." He shook his head, his gaze returning to Max. "Just forget about it."

"I think it's nice for you to have him."

A single bark of laughter burst out of Crane, visibly startling Gabriela. "Ha," he said, bitterness blunting the single syllable. "Sure. *Nice*."

Gabriela wrinkled her brow at him. "I think he really cares for you," she said, her tone quietly pensive, but then almost immediately, her expression went sly again. "Plus, that boy's *culo es como un durazno*." She pointed her chin towards Max, with a suggestive look in Crane's direction. "He's very handsome . . . I'd be *happy* to be getting with that."

"Really? You're just going to rub it in my face?" Crane winced inwardly at his peevish tone, but he couldn't help it.

"What do you mean?"

"That you two are, you *know* . . ." He gestured vaguely, unable to bring himself to say it out loud.

It apparently took a few seconds for Gabriela to grasp his meaning—her brows slowly met in the centre of her forehead, forming a steep, perplexed arc. Then, she let out a sharp laugh and shook her head.

"*Azo*, no, it's not like that! Not really. He had no interest.

So, *no*, I did not fuck your boy, *chacalón*." Gabriela gave Crane a rueful smile.

"You didn't?" Confused, Crane turned to watch Max chase Gabriela's purple hard case around the moving carousel. If the two of them hadn't had sex, what did she call what they'd been doing, then? And what about the condoms in the wastebasket?

Made you look, Doc.

Crane shook the voice out of his head, then glanced back at the young woman. "Sorry. I thought you had."

"Yes, we only, uh . . . *agasajar* . . . you know, played around? Weed makes me a little"—grimacing, she fanned herself with a hand—"you know, crazy and hot to go. But no, we never fucked." Then, her gaze softened. "I'm sorry. I didn't know you had, uh, a *relacion exclusiva*."

The young woman's apology rang with sincerity, so Crane decided to give her the benefit of the doubt. It wasn't her fault that Max was a pathological liar who delighted in withholding information.

"Thanks," Crane said at length. "It's been bothering me."

"Ah. Well, now you know." Gabriela reached out and clasped his forearm as if to comfort him. Then her smile widened into a cheeky grin. "You know, jealousy can be very bad for your *herramienta*," she said, making her finger dangle limply. "But I'm hearing you don't have that problem?" She cocked an eyebrow at him as she slowly pointed her finger skywards.

Crane had to laugh. "Oh, have you, now?" There was something very disarming about her playful manner. "Hey, Gabi, can I ask you a personal question?"

"Sure."

"How old are you?"

The young woman jerked back in apparent affront and snapped her gum a couple of times before answering. "Don't you know you're not supposed to ask a woman her age? It is *rude*."

"Oh," Crane said, chastened. "Shit, I'm sorry."

"*A poco?*" Gabriela's fierce expression dissolved with her giggle, and she wrinkled her nose teasingly at him. "*Guau*, you're so *easy*."

"What's this now?" Max asked, parking the wheeled suitcase in front of Gabriela with a flourish.

"Your *novio* wants to know how old I am."

"Why . . . you dirty old scoundrel." Squaring his shoulders, Max gave Crane an exaggerated once-over. Then he smiled, dropping the fake English accent. "She's older than I am, Doc."

"Ah," Crane replied. It didn't quite answer the question though—he still didn't know precisely how old Max was.

"I guess this is goodbye then, eh?" Max said, addressing Gabriela. "So, where are you off to?"

"I'm meeting with people I know in Amsterdam. We're hanging about there until the Valhalla electronic musical festival, then I don't know . . . maybe to start looking at universities, I think. Maybe visit my mother in Argentina." She shrugged. "You still going to Paris?"

Max nodded, but it was the first Crane had heard of it. "Come and visit if you're in the neighbourhood," he added and gave her a double cheek-to-cheek air kiss in parting.

"*Claro.*" She smiled.

As Gabriela turned to Crane to look up at him, a tiny wrinkle appeared between her dark, shapely brows. "You know I'm free now? To do normal, fun things . . . you know?" she told him. Then, tilting her head, she narrowed her eyes. "Thank you for helping with that, even though you didn't *know* you were helping. It means so much. More than all this diamonds and gold."

Struck by her solemn expression, he remembered the look she'd worn at her uncle's house. "It's all right." Crane smiled. "It only cost me a finger."

Gabriela then surprised him by looping a hand around the back of his neck to pull him down while going up on tiptoe so their mouths could meet in a soft kiss. Her tongue darted between his lips, touching his briefly before she pulled away with a mischievous grin.

Cheeks hot, Crane decided Max was right—Gabriela *was* a hoot. He rubbed the back of his neck where her hand had rested, uncomfortably aware that Max was watching him in amusement.

"You're free too, eh? Enjoy it." She patted him lightly on the chest. "Bye, *papi*. And . . . take care of that boy."

Take care of *Max*? Crane wanted to argue that if anyone in the world could take care of himself, it was Max. However, she had said it so earnestly that he kept his mouth shut and just nodded.

Gabriela then grabbed the handle of her suitcase, wheeled it around, and threw a breezy *chau* over her shoulder as she left for departures. In a moment, the crowd had swallowed her up, and she was gone. Crane wondered if he'd ever see her again.

"Here, I have something for you."

Still in a slight daze, Crane turned to Max and watched him dig through his messenger bag.

"Okay, *sooo* . . ." Max finally came up with a dog-eared tan envelope and handed it to Crane. "Inside is a credit-slash-debit card in Chuck Noland's name and a sheet with a bunch of numbers on it. *Don't lose it.* It's got the account number and password and a list of security tokens for a tax-free bank account I also opened for you. I've already deposited sixty grand American in there, and I'll deposit the rest once I get it. Then, there's a thousand euros in cash, you know, in case you need money now, and another thousand in the account linked to the card."

"Okay." Crane was mystified. "Thank you? But . . . uh, what's going on? Deposit the rest of what?"

Max blinked slowly at Crane a few times, staring at him like he thought his brain was going in slow motion, which it might be—the flight attendant had been heavy-handed with the whiskey.

"Your half of the cut, Doc."

"What . . . really?" Crane looked up from the envelope, startled.

"Yes, really." Max laughed. "Even steven."

"Oh."

Max adjusted the bag on his shoulder and shrugged. "I just wanted to make sure you knew you don't need to rely on me. Not anymore. You have your own money. You can make your own way. No strings attached."

Weeks back, when Crane threatened to turn himself in, Max said something in the same vein: *I'll give you money. You've got your passport . . . you can travel and live anywhere you want.* But last time, it had come with a promise that Crane would never have to see him again. Was that what was happening now? Was Max setting him free?

Mulling over Max's words, Crane thought about what he might do with the quarter million dollars that was apparently coming to him. He looked away, watching the throngs of tourists and business travellers going by, imagining himself among them, without Max.

"I could just . . . take off?" he asked, studying Max's face.

Max nodded slowly.

"With my own money?"

Another nod.

"No tricks?"

A dimple made a brief appearance. "No tricks."

Now, if only Max could be trusted.

The offer felt like a sort of happily ever after, fully equipped with a handy escape hatch and safety net. It sounded great . . . but it also sounded like a trap.

Frowning, Crane pinched the bridge of his nose and grimaced from the growing pain in his skull. He had no intention of leaving Max, but just knowing that he *could* leave and be able to take care of himself should the situation arise? What *wasn't* there to like? Crane knew he should be more suspicious, but he could barely hold a string of thoughts together—all he really wanted at that moment was to lie down somewhere dark and close his eyes for a bit. His hand had started hurting again, but it was too soon to take another painkiller.

Max said something quietly then, something Crane didn't catch over the thudding racket his pulse was making in his ears.

"Hm?"

"I said, are you coming with me to Paris?" Max's expression was a little guarded.

Visiting Paris had never really appealed to him, even though he and Mary had talked about going on several occasions, *usually* after making up from an argument. However, the thought of being there with Max was . . . compelling? He furrowed his brow. Exciting?

"Hey, while you make up your mind, I have to hit the head," Max said with a wry grin as he cocked his head towards the nearest restroom.

"Oh. Okay." Crane nodded, wincing when the motion caused his brain to slosh about.

"Look." Max pointed across the hallway. "Why don't you go browse a bit? I won't be a moment." He gave Crane a teasing smile. "Maybe they'll actually have something to fit those skis you call feet."

Crane just stared groggily at the brightly lit airport shoe store for a moment. Finding shoes for his size-eleven feet had proven difficult when they'd first arrived in Mexico—the largest size the *zapaterías* carried was a nine. It was only when they had gotten to the Mayan Riviera and its booming tourist trade that they found something to fit him.

Glancing down at his stained shoes, he sighed. "No, I'll look later," Crane said, scrubbing at his face wearily. "My head hurts and my hand hurts and I just want to get to the hotel or wherever we're going . . ." He lifted his head, but Max had already gone.

Crane trudged to the nearest wall and leaned against it, closing his eyes. Despite the pain he was in, he felt hopeful, which was something he hadn't been in a while. They would have money to last them a long time—maybe even enough to keep Max busy and out of trouble. Plus, the cops were no longer a concern.

Smiling faintly, Crane thought about croissants and good wine and little cafés where the waiters would sneer at his terrible French . . . most of all, he thought about how he would enjoy his freedom, just like Gabriela was enjoying hers.

Overall, it felt like a new beginning. What was the thing Audrey Hepburn said in *Sabrina*? Something like, "Paris is for changing your outlook, throwing open the windows, and letting in *la vie en rose*."

Crane cracked open an eye at the sound of approaching footsteps, but unfortunately, it wasn't Max. Looking towards the restrooms, he wondered what was taking him so long. Hopefully, he was all right. He squinted at the fancy wristwatch and saw that it was 11:41 a.m. He decided to give Max another few minutes, just in case his stomach was off from the long flight.

When Crane next looked at his watch and saw it was three minutes to noon, he knew something was wrong. Cursing himself for zoning out, he pushed away from the wall and cut through the hallway traffic to enter the restroom. Save for the lone man at the urinals, it was empty.

FIFTEEN
THE CASTAWAY

SUNDAY, DECEMBER 10TH

Crane sat hunched in the uncomfortable plastic seat, his head on a swivel between the two gates where flights to Paris were leaving from in the next few hours. He was tired and stressed, but most of all, he was starving. But he didn't dare move. It would mean passing the security guard again, and the man was starting to suspect something. Actually, *all* of them were becoming suspicious of his presence. Crane had no idea what the rules were when it came to staying in an airport in a foreign country for an extended period without a boarding pass, and he didn't dare ask.

He looked down at his wrinkled shirt and self-consciously smoothed it down, then finger-combed his hair back, peering over at the nearest gate again, relentlessly searching for any sign of Max. He believed one of two things could have happened to his companion:

The first was that Max had simply up and abandoned him.

The second was that Max had left the bathroom, missing Crane snoozing on his feet nearby, and gone into the shoe store to find him. Then, at the *precise* moment Crane went into the men's room to look for Max, Max had come out of the store, missing him a second time. Presumably, he'd looked for Crane but had had to leave to make his appointment with the buyer.

Crane knew he was being naïve, hoping it was the latter, but he couldn't bring himself to believe Max would just ditch him like that. However, after three days of skulking about the airport, avoiding security while watching every Paris-bound boarding line, Crane knew that that was most likely the case.

There was a third option too. Something his delirious brain had cooked up about the Spanish Mafia—if that was a thing—and the gold coins and people kidnapping Max, but he was trying not to waste his diminishing brainpower on farfetched theories. Besides, no one knew they were in Madrid except the guy Max was selling the coins to and Gabriela and maybe Vivian.

Oh. Maybe the guy buying the coins and Max were attacked by militant Mexican activists because they came to take the coins back to Mexico where they belonged . . . the coins might be Spanish, but they were minted on Mayan gold. Minted on? Minted with?

Crane frowned, turning to give his attention to the other gate for a while.

Wait . . . is the gold Mayan or Aztec? He couldn't remember.

"*Señor?*"

Crane instantly lifted the crumpled newspaper he was

holding, hiding behind it like he was in some terrible spy movie.

"Señor," the man repeated, pushing the newspaper down. It was the security guard from earlier.

"Sorry. *No hablo inglés*," Crane replied and then sighed, mentally kicked himself. He'd meant to say "*Je ne parle pas le espagnole*," in French, which he was almost certain was grammatically incorrect, but it made a hell of a lot more sense than telling a Spanish speaker that he couldn't speak English. "I mean, I don't speak *Spanish*." Crane let out a nervous laugh.

"Then we will converse in English," the security guard replied, his smile coldly polite. "*Señor*, you cannot stay here. You need a boarding pass for a flight today, or you must leave. You have been here too long."

"But I'm looking for someone." Crane glanced quickly at the gates again, afraid he'd missed catching a glimpse of Max because of the distraction. He knew he was in the grip of sleep-deprived lunacy, but he couldn't stop himself. "You don't understand. I *need* to be here."

"If you *must* stay at the airport, there are rooms you can book at the airport hotel. You may put your belongings there . . . have some sleep." The man wrinkled his nose delicately. "Take a shower. Come, I will show you." He gestured for Crane to stand, but Crane just shook his head. "Come, *Señor*."

"No, I can't miss him. This is where I need to be."

The plaintive note in Crane's voice seemed to have an effect on the man—his stern expression faded, and when he spoke next, it was evident that he thought Crane was having some sort of mental health crisis . . . which he supposed he *was*.

"Do you have someone I can call for you?" the man asked gently.

Crane shook his head, rubbing his good hand over the thick stubble on his jaw. "I don't *know* where he is. That's what I'm *trying* to tell you."

Then his eyes widened, and he fished out the receipt he'd found in his breast pocket. He didn't know when Gabriela had slipped it to him, probably when she had given him that kiss, but it had come fluttering out yesterday when he'd bent over to pick up his bag. Written on the blank side in a girlish hand was:

gabi.espada94@gmail.com – If you need me.

Crane handed the slip of paper to the security guard. "I need to email this person."

Standing in Charles de Gaulle airport five hours later, Crane tried to figure out the fare for the subway to Paris. Problem was, Paris turned out to be a lot bigger and more complicated than he'd expected, and until Gabriela answered his email, he had no idea where to go. And even *that* was hinging on the young woman knowing where Max's apartment was in Paris.

Since Max had neglected to give Crane the PIN for the card he'd given him, he'd paid cash for his plane ticket to Paris. The ticket had cost only €150, but along with the hundred he'd spent eating at the airport over the past three days, the fifteen for a new clean shirt, plus another thirty to get a pass to the VIP lounge where he'd taken a shower, he had €700 left in cash in the envelope and around five in change in his pocket.

Crane decided Central Paris was where he should go. Chances are, that was where the tourist area was, and hopefully, he wouldn't have too much trouble finding an internet café to check his email.

He squinted at the ticketing information again. It looked like it was around ten euros, so he pulled a twenty out of the envelope and bought a one-way ticket on the RER train headed for Central Paris.

The subway car ended up being a little crowded, but Crane managed to find a seat. The helpful attendant at the airport station had told him that the trip to the Paris Gare du Nord station would take roughly half an hour, so he set a timer on Preston's fancy watch, put his bag down between his feet, crossed his arms over his chest, and continued the nap he had started on the flight from Madrid.

Crane woke with a snort when the alarm on his watch went off. Blearily looking around, he realized they were coming up on a station, but was it the one he wanted?

There was an announcement over the speakers, but it was as crackly and unintelligible as the ones in the Montréal metro system. Thankfully, there was a lit panel above the door showing the stations in real-time—Gare du Nord was the one after next.

Anxious to get off the train and begin his search, Crane reached down for his bag. . . and found nothing. His heart stopped. Hoping he had just kicked it back in his sleep, he crouched down and looked under the seat and the next seat over in case it had slid. The dark-blue backpack was nowhere to be found.

Panicking, Crane began asking everyone around him if they had seen his bag.

"*Pardonez-moi, tu as . . . voir . . .* uh, *mon sac?* You know . . . um, a backpack? *Sac à dos? Monsieur? Madame? Mon sac à dos* was stolen."

The people who weren't actively ignoring him mostly shook their heads and averted their eyes. A few took pity on him and helped him search, but as the train rolled into his station, he had to admit that the bag was gone.

"Stupid," Crane rasped to himself, his breathing ragged from his speeding pulse. He felt faint from shock. "Fucking stupid."

He had all of fifteen euros to his name, no identification, nothing. What was he going to do? Crane waited for the version of Max that lived in his head to comment, but that voice had gone silent days ago, apparently abandoning him as well.

Following the crowd, Crane finally emerged from the station and just stood there in a daze on the street, wondering what the hell he should do. It was dark and freezing out, and he was severely underdressed and had nowhere to go.

After spending the next hour walking and asking for Central Paris while getting sent in all different directions, Crane finally sat down on a cold bench, put his face in his hands, and wept.

○

TUESDAY, DECEMBER 12TH

Crane handed his watch to the white-haired man behind the counter and looked around the shop while the man inspected it. The glass display cases to either side were filled with gold and silver jewellery and high-end watches. In the centre of the room was a tall case laden with silver teapots and serving dishes, gold-rimmed wineglasses and sophisticated-looking cut crystal goblets. He clasped his hands behind his back, pretending avid interest in a set of 24-carat gold spoons.

It was just nice to get out of the cold.

Thankfully, Paris was a city that was relatively kind to its homeless population. There were several emergency shelters where he could stay the night and *Restaurants du Coeurs* that served food to anyone in need. He'd even been given a good coat and a hat by the woman running the shelter near Notre-Dame de Paris.

Unfortunately, while begging wasn't illegal in France, it was actively discouraged in the more upscale neighbourhoods of Paris—and that's where he needed to be.

Gabriela had finally answered his email the previous day, writing that while she didn't know precisely where Max lived, she had heard him mention that his flat was in Gros-Caillou, which was in the 7th *arrondissement*, a city demarcation which Crane took to be similar to the boroughs of Montréal. If the 16th *arrondissement* was like Westmount, the wealthiest part of Montréal island, and where Max's mother and step-father lived, then the 7th or *le septième* was probably akin to the area of Montréal where the Museum of Arts was or maybe parts of Old Montreal.

Crane had soon realized he'd need money to get himself back and forth from the shelter to Gros-Caillou every day to search for Max, and because all the places serving free food were far from there, he'd need money to eat as well. Then, he had remembered what Max had said about Preston's watch.

Hopefully, it would fetch a few thousand, which was more than enough to keep him going for a while.

Walking over to one of the low counters, Crane peered through the glass at a pearl-encrusted hair comb.

It was amazing how calm he felt about everything now that his shock and horror had played out and he'd accepted his situation. Now, all he had to do was keep searching for Max until his money and luck ran out, and when that inevitably happened, he'd head to the Canadian Embassy and tell them who he was. Then, at least he'd get to die in jail instead of on the streets of Paris. Easy peasy.

Of course, the heavy painkillers were definitely contributing to his nonchalance . . . or was that fatalism?

That morning, Crane had gone to a free clinic where they had rebandaged his hand and given him enough pills to last two weeks. He'd already given two of those away in thanks to the man who panhandled outside the falafel place nearest the Petit Pont—if it wasn't for Miloud that first night in Paris,

Crane might already be dead. Hypothermia was no laughing matter.

Another few minutes passed before the shop owner called him over, placing the watch on the counter in front of him.

"*Izafeck*," the man said, pointing to the watch.

Crane frowned at the man. "Iz . . . afeck?" he asked, wondering what it meant. It didn't sound French. Maybe it was Arabic? The man looked a little like Miloud, who was from Morroco.

After making a harsh noise in the back of his throat, the shopkeeper repeated himself. "Izafeck!" He made as if to push the watch towards Crane with both hands. "Iz. A. Feck."

"I'm sorry. I don't understand what you're saying."

The shopkeeper grunted, stroking down his thick white moustache with a gnarled hand while muttering a few words to himself in French. Crane thought he heard *Américain*.

"Iz not, *euh . . . genuine*," the man said at last.

"Ohhh," Crane replied, finally cluing in. "It's a *fake*!" Then the words sunk in. "Wait, it's a fake?" He picked up the watch and peered closely at it. "Are you sure?"

"Iz a fake, yes," the old man said, sitting up on his stool.

Crane was confused. Had Preston been having money issues? Why would he have a fake watch? Was he just . . . cheap? Maybe Preston didn't even know it was counterfeit? On the other hand, maybe it was a fluke and Crane, with his *incredible* luck, had picked the only fake in the lot.

"All right. But it's got to be worth *something*, right?" he asked.

"I give forty euros."

Staring down at the watch in bitter disappointment, Crane sighed, kicking himself for getting his hopes up.

"Can you do a little higher? Like . . . fifty?" He could stretch it out by eating only in the evenings, saving the money for the metro trips. At least the *sanisettes*—the little automatic bathroom stalls scattered around the city—were free to use.

The shop owner crossed his arms over his sunken chest and raised one eyebrow, turning his high forehead into a tightly ridged landscape. "Thirty."

Shit. "I'm sorry. *Je suis désolé.*" He clasped his hands in front of him. "Forty is fine. I'll take forty." Crane cleared his throat. "Please," he said softly, "I'm desperate."

The old man gave him a curt nod, then took the watch and swivelled around on his stool, dropping it in a small cardboard box on the shelf behind him. Then, turning back to fix Crane with a stern look, the shop owner opened the register and handed Crane a crisp fifty.

Crane stared at the bill for a few seconds. "I'm sorry. I don't have change."

The shop owner just made a shooing gesture, his brow furrowed, and Crane let out a sharp breath, holding the bill to his chest with both hands as he realized what was happening.

"*Merci, monsieur. Merci.*"

The man snorted, his surly expression never changing, and turned his back to Crane, flapping a hand over his shoulder, dismissing him.

Laughing softly, Crane pocketed the money. "*Merci.*"

○

SATURDAY, DECEMBER 16TH

Crane held the paper coffee cup in both hands, warming them as he blew softly across the top.

Across the street, a dinged-up green car was trying to fit into a parking spot for a much smaller vehicle. Crane shook his head in amusement as the driver gently pushed the car's bumper ahead of him to make more space. It wasn't the first time he'd witnessed such a thing—it seemed expected for drivers not to use their parking brakes. Karim had jokingly called the manoeuvre a "French kiss."

He frowned, looking to his left where he could see the top of the Eiffel Tower poking above one of the wedge-shaped buildings found at almost every intersection in the city.

Hm.

Karim was late. Maybe he'd finally asked the girl in his sauces class to go to coffee with him.

Crane had befriended the young Algerian a few days earlier when he'd been walking up and down Rue Saint-Dominique, begging for change so he could fill the terrible pit in his stomach. Karim had stopped and given him two euro coins from his pocket, then, when hearing his terrible French, had asked him if he was American.

On learning Crane was Canadian, the affable young man had peppered him with all sorts of questions about the differences between France French and French in Québec, something Crane sheepishly admitted not knowing much about. Undeterred, Karim had continued asking questions, explaining that he planned on eventually moving to Québec once he finished his studies.

Coincidentally, Karim was enrolled at *Le Cordon Bleu*,

the same school where Max was theoretically going, and Crane wondered whether Karim knew the student who was taking Max's place. He would ask him when he showed up today.

Usually, Karim walked through the area where Crane had set up watch—an intersection that got a lot of foot traffic at the edge of Gros-Caillou, the area Max was supposed to be living —but there was no sign of him yet.

Crane sighed, shifting from foot to foot as he pulled up the collar of his coat to better cover his ears. It was warmer than it had been for the past week, but it was only around 10°C. He was still wearing the canvas running shoes he'd bought in Playa del Carmen, the bloodstain now just a faded splotch, and they were not well suited to the cold. He couldn't remember the last time his feet had been warm. Worse, someone had nicked his wool hat on Thursday, and he hadn't yet found a replacement.

Oh right. It's Saturday, he remembered. So there would be no Karim to have a friendly chat with and no spare coins. *Ah well.* He'd made a little money panhandling earlier, enough to buy the coffee he was drinking and maybe a falafel pita to eat for lunch tomorrow.

He took a scalding sip from his cup, squinting at the oncoming pedestrians. The sun was going down, and the city would soon sparkle with Christmas lights. The glittering décor definitely made the hour's walk back to the shelter more pleasant.

Overall, Crane thought being homeless wasn't *terrible* exactly, and out of all the cities where he could have found himself, Paris was probably a good place to be. It was cold but not brutally so, it felt safe to walk around, there were many social programs to help people in his situation . . . and it was pretty.

Crane smiled, drinking more coffee as he watched the Eiffel Tower's lights go on. He'd stick around for another half hour, then start the journey back. Crane decided he'd stop halfway and try his luck around *Le Bon Marché*. The department store was crowded with holiday shoppers . . . maybe someone would take pity on him.

Once the sky was dark, Crane threw his cup in the trash and headed toward "home." He got less than six blocks before the group of teenagers converged on him.

DECEMBER . . . ?

Crane held out the cup with a trembling hand, holding the blanket together with the other, his bandage dirty and frayed. He nodded his thanks to the woman who gave him a few coins, then hunched his shoulders and waited for the next person to pass.

His eye was getting better—he could open it now at least —and his ribs didn't hurt quite as much today, but he was frozen to the bone. The weather was barely above freezing, and the thin coat he'd received to replace the one stolen did nothing to warm his bones, nor did the scratchy blanket he'd traded the last of his painkillers for.

He'd go back to the clinic . . . when he found the strength to get there.

Crane had managed to find his way back to the shelter after the beating, only to discover they'd given his bed away because of the late hour. The nice folks who ran the place tried to find him space in one of the other emergency shelters scattered around the city, but because of the holiday season, everyone was packed to capacity. He'd spent the last few nights sharing the hard floor with a dozen other itinerants, a terrifically uncomfortable way to sleep when you're both injured and thin to the point of emaciation.

Coughing, he extended the cup once more, but this time no change was forthcoming from the couple passing by.

Crane knew it was the end of this foolish venture. He'd never find Max. There was nothing left but to pack it up and present himself to the authorities at the Canadian embassy— at least he'd be warm and fed in jail.

Shivering, he rested his blanket-covered head against the cold bricks and closed his eyes.

Yes . . . the clinic and then the embassy, he thought. But first, a little nap.

O

"Doc?"

Crane's body felt heavy and numb. Even his eyelids weighed a thousand pounds. He struggled to lift them.

"Doc? Come on, Doc. Look at me."

Finally, the darkness split apart, letting in a hazy light. He peered at the blurry face in front of him, confused.

"Am I dead?" His voice was just a low croak.

The apparition smiled, Max's features coming into focus.

"Jesus Christ, Doc. You had me scared for a second. No, you're not dead, just dead cold."

"Max?"

Chuckling, Max rubbed his hands quickly up and down Crane's biceps, warming him.

"Yeah, it's me, Doc. I found you."

"You did?"

"I did. Now let's get you home."

Suddenly Crane couldn't see Max very well. His eyes were too full of tears.

SIXTEEN
THE OLD FAMILIAR TUNE

MONDAY, JANUARY 1ST

Crane smiled sleepily and stretched before burrowing deeper into the fluffy white bedding, trying to block out the bright winter sun streaming through the floor-to-ceiling windows of Max's apartment.

He wasn't exactly sure how many days it had been since Max found him sleeping on the street, but it felt like a lifetime ago.

"There you are, sleepyhead." Max pulled the duvet from Crane's face. "I grabbed us some *pains aux chocolats* from downstairs and made coffee. Are you getting out of bed? It's past noon."

Groaning softly, Crane cracked one eye open and tried pulling the sheet over his head, but Max stopped him with a laugh, leaning down to kiss him on the tip of his nose.

"Come *on*." Max shook him roughly. "You need to get out of here so the maid can clean."

"I can't believe you're making that poor girl work on New

Year's Day," Crane replied, relinquishing his hold on the bedding. He sat up and ran a hand through his hair, blinking against the sunlight reflecting on all the white surfaces.

"Well, I'm paying her plenty," Max replied, throwing a black T-shirt at Crane.

"I don't get why she has to clean in here." Crane pulled the shirt over his head. It hung on him like a sail. It would take weeks to put on the weight he'd lost. "It's not like your mother's going to come in here."

The plan was for Crane to hide out in the bedroom, pretending to be a sick roommate, while Mrs. Ouimet paid Max a visit. She and her husband Marc had attended a glamorous New Year's Eve party in Paris the night before and were leaving that day to spend the rest of the week in Alsace. The visit would be brief, thankfully, since Marc wouldn't come and wasn't willing to wait too long at the hotel.

"She might pop her head 'round just to take a look," Max replied. "She's nosy. Just put your face under the pillow or something if you hear her coming." He smiled at Crane, then furrowed his brow, wagging his finger. "And *no* killing her this time."

Laughing, Crane shook his head, pulling him in for a quick kiss.

He still couldn't believe that Max had actually found him. It was amazing that out of all the people Max could have talked to the day he went to the cooking school to pick up some paperwork, it was Karim he'd struck up a conversation with. When Karim mentioned having met another man from Montréal, one who was living on the streets and who didn't speak French, Max had quickly surmised by his physical description that it was Crane.

The young man had visited all the homeless shelters and *Restaurants du Coeurs*, finally happening upon Crane sleeping on the stoop of a bakery.

Max had proclaimed it a Christmas miracle. Crane was just happy he'd been found before he'd given himself up . . . or died.

And Max *hadn't* abandoned him in the airport as he'd assumed. The truth was closer to the other scenario Crane had come up with. Max had used the restroom but had gotten turned around on exiting, following a tall thin man who resembled Crane from behind. When he had discovered his error, he had retraced his steps, but at that point, Crane had gone in the other direction to search for him.

Angry and confused, and assuming Crane had decided to ditch him, Max had gone to his meeting with the museum representative to sell the coins. Then, he'd taken the fancy overnight train to Paris he'd booked the two of them. The trip had been meant as a surprise—a luxury cabin of their own with gourmet meals and champagne to celebrate. Max said he had spent most of the nine-and-a-half hours composing an email that Crane had never even received. When Crane had gone to email Gabriela from the airport in Madrid, he'd had to create a new email address—the password to his old one was stored on Max's computer.

A few hours later, Crane was back in the bedroom, one arm tucked behind his head as he read from Max's Kindle. Downstairs, Max's mother was chatting excitedly with a cousin who had accompanied her to the flat.

Hearing the floor creak outside the door, Crane quickly

put the device down and turned his head towards the window. A sliver of the Eiffel Tower was visible between two Art Nouveau buildings up the street.

"It's just me. I wanted to check in and see how you were doing."

"I'm fine." Crane smiled at Max. "I thought she was only staying an hour."

"Yeahhhh, well . . . that's my mom for you. She and my aunt brought some stuff to make flower arrangements to 'beautify' the place, and it's like a whole production, I swear." Max rolled his eyes. "Marc is probably sitting there in the hotel room *fuming*." He sat up and grinned. "Hey, I've got an idea." Going up on his knees, Max undid the fly of his skinny jeans before throwing himself on his back on the bed to wiggle out of them.

"What are you *doing*?" Crane stared at Max.

He was down to just the tight dark-grey T-shirt with a single red balloon floating on the front.

"Think we have time for a quickie before they notice I'm gone?"

"Uh."

Apart from one failed tipsy attempt two days prior, they hadn't been intimate since Crane's rescue. Max thought it was just exhaustion, but Crane wasn't convinced. But, whether physical or psychological, the only thing for sure was that his dick wasn't happy about something.

Max straddled Crane's lap, his eyes heavy-lidded and his smile seductive as he jiggled his hips from side to side to elicit a response.

"Don't you want to fuck me?" Max asked, biting the corner of his lip as he studied Crane's face.

With a chuckle, Crane clasped Max's waist between his hands. His left hand was no longer bandaged—the skin was still raw and pink where his finger had been cut off, and it ached and itched from time to time, but it was more or less healed.

"I do," Crane replied honestly. He pushed his pelvis up into Max, willing his dick to get hard, but nothing was happening. "I think I just need a little more time."

Right then, the door opened, and Crane flung his head to the side, pulling up the edge of the duvet to cover his face.

"Pumpkin?" Mrs. Ouimet said, stepping into the room.

Crane felt rather than heard Max's annoyed growl over being interrupted.

"*Mom.* Can't you see I'm a little busy here?"

"Oh." She was silent for several seconds, which was long, considering she could clearly see that her son was naked from the waist down. "Well, hurry up," she finally said with a dismissive laugh. "You have to give *un bec* to *Matante* Gisèle before she leaves. Then I have to go back and get your father before he has too many drinks at the bar."

Crane felt Max's body tense.

"He's not my father."

"Whatever. Just come down," she said airily, then pitched her voice higher to cheerfully add, "Hello, Édouard's roommate. I hope you feel better soon!"

Waving his hand in the general direction of her voice, Crane heard Mrs. Ouimet leave. He pulled the sheet from his face and frowned at the still-open bedroom door.

"Goodness gracious," Max said, climbing off Crane. "That woman."

He walked over to the chest of drawers and tugged one

open, plucking out a pair of white lace panties. Grinning at Crane, he slowly pulled them up, tucking his cock and balls neatly into the front where they made the delicate material bulge lewdly.

Max winked, turning around. "Now you have something to think about while I go take care of our guests."

Crane's eyes traced the line of the dark furrow between Max's cheeks, clearly visible through the white lace, and nodded.

"Be right back." Max stepped into his tight jeans, jumping in place a few times to get them on all the way, then tossed a coy look over his shoulder before he left the room.

Chuckling, Crane squeezed his dick through his pants. It wasn't actually hard . . . but neither was it completely soft. It was a start.

Impatient for Max to return, Crane picked up the Kindle again, only to see it was running low on batteries.

"Dammit."

He slid off the bed, wondering where Max kept the charger. It wasn't in the single bedside table, nor was it on the top of the dresser. Crane could have sworn he'd seen a cable lying around the room before, but the maid had tidied up, so now it could be anywhere.

He opened the top drawer of the dresser where Max had found the panties and smirked at the collection of frilly and lacy items he found within. Amused and getting more than a little aroused, he lifted a satiny dark-purple thong out of the drawer and shook his head.

If someone had told him years ago that this is what he would end up doing—snooping through his boyfriend's panty drawer and getting a boner—he would have walked out of the room and probably avoided them in the future.

Crane put the thong back and dug through the pile, curious about what else was in there. When he found a stack of Polaroids at the bottom of the drawer, Crane fully expected them to be of a salacious nature. However, there was nothing dirty about the photos.

A few depicted a group of small children around a table—there was a cake in front of a very young boy with dark hair. Was that Max? Crane squinted, wishing they'd made it to the optometrist before everything closed for the holidays. The eye strain couldn't be good for him.

He flipped through the rest of the Polaroids. They were mainly of the birthday party, with a few shots of a canoe trip thrown in. The last photo in the pile could have belonged to the party too, but it was hard to tell. It was a picture of a man with the same dark-haired boy from the cake photo. The little boy sat on the man's lap clutching a stuffed animal—a spotted cat—and both the man and the boy were beaming at the camera.

Narrowing his eyes, Crane studied the photo as Max's words echoed in his head:

I thought I was getting the stuffed toy cheetah I saw at the store. Instead, he told me I was old enough to start playing a new game.

Crane took a better look at the toy in the photograph. Yes, definitely a cheetah, given the black "tears" below its eyes.

But . . . Crane furrowed his brow, rubbing his fingertips back and forth over his lips. Was the man in the photo Max's real dad? Bearded and wearing a blue flannel shirt, the man did *look* like a truck driver. But what did it mean that he had given Max a cheetah? In the fabricated story Max had told him about getting molested by his father, but he didn't get the cheetah in the end.

You know, he did give me a stuffed teddy bear afterwards, but I wanted a cheetah. A cheetah.

Crane flipped the photo over. On the back, written in faded blue ink, was:

Michel & Eddie

There was no date.

For a brief moment, it was like two versions of the little boy existed simultaneously. One boy had received a teddy bear for his pain, and the other, a cheetah for his joy. Eddie and Max . . . Max and Eddie. Was there any truth to the story Max had told him after all?

Nah, Doc . . . You're just looking for excuses for why I am the way I am. It was the first time since Crane arrived in Paris that he'd heard Max's voice in his head.

Unnerved, Crane quickly slid the stack of Polaroids back

under the pile of lingerie and, in doing so, knocked a pair of bright-red panties to the floor.

"Shit." He bent down to pick them up and froze, his eyes locked on a dark-blue strap sticking out from a canvas storage box on the bottom shelf of the bookcase.

No.

He straightened, distractedly closing the drawer, his gaze still on the strap. The colour was the right shade of blue—not navy, not royal . . . somewhere exactly between the two.

No.

Sitting down on the edge of the bed, Crane scratched the back of his head, reasoning with himself—*no*, it couldn't possibly be what he thought it was. It was *definitely* something else.

The only way to know for sure, however, was to look.

"No." He said it aloud as if *that* could keep him safe from confirming his worst fear. It was no good. Crane knew he had to look.

With one ear to the chatter downstairs, Crane knelt in front of the bookcase, rubbing his hands together as if priming them to touch something loathsome. Then he slowly reached out and lifted the top off the soft-sided storage box.

"Jesus." It came out as a hoarse whisper, the sudden drop of his heart to the pit of his stomach stealing his voice.

Gently, he lifted the day pack out of the box, handling it like a frail, newborn creature, and set it on the floor in front of him. It didn't *have* to be the bag he'd taken from Preston's room aboard the yacht. It could be someone else's dark-blue backpack of the same model. With the same frayed zipper-pull ribbon on the same front pouch.

He took a deep breath and held his hand above the bag

with a wordless prayer. Then, in one swift motion, like he was ripping off a Band-Aid, he unzipped the bag.

Max stopped in his tracks when he saw Crane sitting motionless on the bed, the blue backpack in his lap. His gaze flicked to the envelope, cash, Canadian passport, and bank card Crane had carefully laid out on the bed beside him.

"I think we need to have a little chat," Crane said, his voice calm. "Don't we?"

"About what?" Max took a step back, his giggle high and nervous.

"Wrong answer."

Lunging to his feet, Crane grabbed for Max but missed, and Max let out another peal of laughter and bolted for the stairs. Crane chased after him, nearly tripping on the last step down, and jumped over the back of the couch, his long legs giving him the advantage. He cornered Max briefly in the small dining room, but Max evaded him by ducking beneath the table and making a break for the front door to the flat.

"No, you don't." Crane jumped and caught Max's wrist, only to have him twist in his grasp and escape a second later.

"Too slow!" Max taunted, giggling as he raced back toward the living room.

Letting out a growl of frustration, Crane ran in the direction of the windows, intending to trap Max in that corner of the room, then feinted to the left when Max tried to pass him and finally tackled him to the floor where they landed on the antique rug with a bone-shaking crash.

"No!" Max yelled. Squirming in Crane's grasp, he almost shrieked with laughter, red-faced with his efforts to break free as Crane held him down. He let out a yelp when Crane grabbed a handful of his hair, then gasped in pain, his hands flying to Crane's wrist as Crane tightened his grip.

"You abandoned me in Madrid," Crane said, trying to keep his voice steady despite how hard he was breathing. He used his free hand to grasp Max's nipple, twisting it painfully.

"Ow, *fuck*." Max flailed at him, but Crane slapped his hands away.

Crane stared down at him and repeated, "You abandoned me in Madrid."

"Yes! Yes, I did." Panting through clenched teeth, Max glared up at him.

"You stole my bag." This time, Crane didn't wait to give Max a second chance to answer and just gave his other nipple a sharp twist.

Max let out a squeal, his ribs sharply outlined through his tight T-shirt as he arched his back in pain.

"Yes," he rasped when Crane released him, then let out another uneasy giggle. "I did."

"And you left me to die penniless and pathetic on the streets of Paris," Crane growled.

Before Max could reply, Crane undid the button on the young man's jeans, then yanked the fly open. Grabbing a handful of waistband to each side, he got to his feet, dragging the jeans with him, turning Max half upside down while essentially shaking him out of his tight pants.

When he'd managed to peel the jeans off Max's legs, he grabbed him by the hair again, forcing him to flip over onto his stomach. Then, it was easy enough to put a knee between Max's thighs, hook a finger into the white lace, and rip a hole in the seat of his panties.

"Doc? What are you . . ." Max let out a sharp gasp when Crane cracked him across the ass with the back of his hand.

Pulling his stiff, throbbing dick out of his pants, Crane saw his fury was making him literally drip in anticipation. With a maniacal grin, he forced Max's thighs apart, spat on his cock, and drove it through the jagged rent in the lace.

Max cried out as he was breached, his hands scrabbling for purchase on the woven rug. He moaned, his eyes crushed closed as Crane began to fuck him hard and fast.

It didn't take long before Crane was skirting the edge, the sweat pouring down his back as he pistoned his cock as far as it would go into Max's hole. Covering Max's body with his own, Crane wrapped one arm under Max's throat in a choke hold, then pushed his face into the side of Max's neck, taking his flesh between his teeth to bite down hard as he jerked with the first burst of orgasm.

Max whimpered and gasped, struggling beneath Crane as his ass was flooded with cum, his cries growing quieter as Crane's thrusts slowed and finally stopped.

A minute passed before Crane could breathe again, and he turned over, pulling free of Max to lie on his back on the carpet next to him, all the tension having leaked out of him through his balls.

"Welcome back," Max said quietly.

Crane sighed, rubbing his face. "I should fucking hate you."

"Yeah. You're kind of . . . *uh*, funny that way." Max gave a soft laugh. "Maybe you should see a therapist."

With a dry chuckle, Crane closed his eyes.

After a moment, he glanced over at Max. "Max, *why* did

you do it? Will you tell me that much?" He shook his head slowly. "Was it just for shits and giggles?"

Max gnawed on his bottom lip, his expression going dark as he stared at Crane.

Crane frowned. "What is it?"

Clearing his throat, Max turned to look at the ceiling, waiting a few seconds before answering.

"You hesitated," Max said in a small voice.

Pushing himself up on his elbows, Crane peered over at Max.

Max's eyes flicked to him before returning their focus to the decorative ceiling tiles. "When I asked if you were coming with me to Paris, you hesitated."

"Well, do you *blame* me?" Crane asked, sitting up. "After everything you've put me through, don't you think a little hesitation is called for?"

Max gave a quiet snort but still wouldn't look at him.

"What? Your feelings got all hurt because I didn't jump immediately at the chance to keep following you like a well-trained dog?"

This time, Max turned to face him, his expression cold.

"I was *nice* to you. I gave you money. I gave you a passport. I said you could leave if you wanted to. I thought you'd be *grateful*."

"Grateful?" Crane barked out a laugh. He held up his left hand. "*You cut off my fucking finger.* Excuuuse me for not wanting to kiss your fucking feet for giving me my fair share."

Max blinked slowly at him a few times, then sat up, his mouth set in a hard line.

The two of them sat there glaring at each other in silence.

Finally, Crane spoke up, his voice quiet. "I was hungover. I had a headache."

Max's brows quirked up the tiniest bit. "When?"

"When you asked me if I was coming to Paris with you. I didn't *hesitate*—I had a headache. My brain was like mush." He breathed out slowly. "It's not like I wasn't going to come with you, you asshole . . . My responses were just slow, and you're an impatient little shit."

"Oh."

"Yeah," Crane said, scoffing. "Oh."

"Huh."

Crane tilted his head, watching the crease grow between Max's dark brows. "I really did hurt your feelings, didn't I."

"No." Max looked down at his hands. "It was just inconvenient."

Crane snorted. "Inconvenient enough that you had someone steal my bag? That you orchestrated all this to punish me?" He frowned. "Did you have someone following me around?"

After a moment, Max nodded. "A few someones."

"Karim?"

Max nodded again.

"Does he even go to that school?"

"Doc, he's the one who's been taking courses for me."

Scowling, Crane felt like a complete idiot. "And Miloud? Him too? Yeah? What about the man at the pawn shop? *Jesus.*" He then curled his lip, leaning forward. "Did you pay those fucking kids to beat me up?"

This time Max's eyes went wide. "No. That wasn't me. That wasn't part of the plan. I swear."

"And what *was* the plan? That I'd get so desperate that I'd fall into your arms when you 'rescued' me?"

Max's expression split instantly into a wide grin. "Well, it worked, didn't it?"

Crane looked up at the ceiling, shaking his head. He didn't know what to say or how to feel. On the one hand, he was furious over the betrayal. On the other? Resignation? Ambivalence? Wait, no, was that an odd sense of . . . relief? Curiosity? No, could that be . . . hope?

What the fuck is wrong *with me?*

"Honestly, I don't know why I should stay with you," he said out loud, turning to Max. "You're going to fuck me over the minute I either annoy you or bore you."

Max's eyes went flinty as he studied Crane. "What if I promised not to."

"That's not good enough. You have to *prove* it to me."

"How?"

"You tell me. How can I trust you? Make me believe it."

Max's eyes went distant as he pondered Crane's request, then his brow wrinkled, and he looked up, casting about for something. Max's gaze finally settled on the kitchen counter where his mother and aunt had left their elaborate floral arrangements. He got to his feet and crossed the room to fetch a pair of pruning shears, then turned to Crane.

Wearing nothing but the tight black T-shirt, torn white panties, and a serious expression, Max gestured for Crane to follow him upstairs. He then climbed onto the bed.

"What are we doing?" Crane asked, putting a knee up on the mattress. He looked warily at the shears in Max's hand.

"I'm giving you what you want." Max lifted his backside to slide the lace panties down, discarding them by the bed, and then patted the space between his thighs. "Lose the pants and come here."

Mystified and a little nervous, Crane did as he was told and joined Max on the bed. Max set the shears aside and took hold of Crane's cock, stroking him softly.

It didn't take long for Crane to start getting hard. Max's confessed betrayal had requickened his appetite, and when Max released him to lay back against the pillows, lifting his knees to display his pink cum-slick pucker, it only whetted his hunger further.

Without having to be told, Crane slipped his cock inside Max, fucking him slowly for a dozen strokes before Max stopped him with a raised hand.

Brow wrinkled in confusion, Crane accepted the shears from Max—his heart gave a quick double beat, making him light-headed as he stared down at the sharp tool in his hand.

"What are we doing?" Crane repeated.

Max held out his left hand to Crane. "I'm making you a promise."

It took a second for Max's meaning to percolate into his brain. "You want me to . . . cut your finger off?" he asked slowly.

A nervous grin flashed across Max's face. "Well, *want* isn't exactly the right word." He looked pale, his lips almost bloodless as he stared up at Crane. "But, this is me proving to you that you can trust me."

Crane stared at Max's hand. A normal, sane person would probably refuse the offer. They'd most likely be sickened by it. Instead, Crane's cock stirred inside Max, throbbing in time to Crane's quick but steady heartbeat as it stiffened further. There was nothing he could do to hide his excitement.

"Are you certain?" he whispered, then cleared his throat.

"Yep." Max smiled serenely. "If it means you'll stay with me."

"Okay." Crane nodded, feeling breathless. "You won't abandon me again?" He locked eyes with Max. "Not in jail . . . nowhere?"

Solemnly nodding, Max wrapped his legs around Crane's waist. "Promise."

Crane carefully placed the open shears around the base of Max's left ring finger, intending on cutting it right at the joint as his had been.

"W-wait," Max said. "I want to know . . ."

"What?"

"I want to know that you won't hesitate."

At first, Crane thought Max was referring to the imminent amputation, but then realized he was talking about what had happened at the airport in Madrid. His inferred hesitation had really affected the young man. Crane's expression softened, and he reached out, swiping his thumb across Max's cheek as he cupped the back of his head.

"Nope. You're stuck with me."

Max smiled.

Preparing to close the shears, Crane took a few steadying breaths. "Are you ready?"

Nodding quickly, Max shut his eyes.

"Do you want something to bite down on?"

Cracking open one eye, Max glared balefully. "Jesus, will you just get on—"

His words ended in a scream as the sharp shears crunched easily through flesh and bone.

Crane gasped, his cock squeezed so tight when Max's

body went rigid with pain, then let out a moan as Max's shuddering cries stimulated him further. He started thrusting slowly into him again, watching the blood run down Max's arm to bloom like a red rose on the crisp white sheets beneath his elbow.

Going quiet, Max looked up at him through the tears spilling from his eyes, his lips pulled back against his teeth as he panted. He clutched at his wrist, his arms trembling.

"What?" Crane asked, holding himself in place. He could feel every tremor in Max's body, a heady vibration that intensified his pleasure.

"I didn't think you'd actually do it," Max said, his voice rough. "I didn't think you'd have the fucking balls."

"Hey, this is what you wanted." Crane tilted his head, gazing down at Max. "Here." He pulled his T-shirt off and handed it to Max, who immediately pressed it against his wound to staunch the blood. "Now shut up, I'm not done fucking you."

Max's face was the picture of anguish as more tears streamed down his cheeks, the first real tears he'd ever seen him cry. "Jesus, that's *cold*, Doc."

"You made me this way," Crane said quietly. "I thought you'd be happy."

Red-rimmed and swollen from crying, Max's eyes widened, and then he let out a wail as Crane braced himself on the mattress to either side of his head, driving himself into Max hard.

SEVENTEEN
THE END?

MONDAY, JANUARY 1ST

"Are you sure you don't want to go to the hospital?" Crane asked, scrubbing his fingers lightly through Max's dark curls as he drowsed against his chest.

"Nah, I'm good, *papi*," Max said sleepily. "I feel fine." He was obviously blissed-out from the OxyContin Crane had found in the recovered backpack.

Crane inspected Max's hand. The bandaging he'd done wasn't terribly neat, unlike the near-professional job Max had done on his hand, but it would do. "Can I get you anything?"

"Mmm . . ." Max clicked his tongue a few times, thinking. "Can you go to Thierry's before he closes and get us some vino?"

"I don't think you should be drinking on painkillers," he said gently.

"You did."

Chuckling, Crane nodded. "Touché." He carefully

235

transferred Max from his shoulder to the pillow and made sure he was comfortable. "Anything in particular?"

"Surprise me." Max closed his eyes and let out a contented little mewl when Crane kissed his lips softly.

"I'll guess I'll use my card for once." Crane pulled on a pair of dark-grey slacks, not bothering with any boxers. "Hey, you never gave me the PIN."

Max's lids lifted slowly. "I didn't? It's my birthday—day, month, two digits of the year."

Crane frowned and stopped midway through putting on his shirt. "I don't know when your birthday is."

"Oh." Brow deeply furrowed, Max stared at Crane. "Is that why you never got me a present?"

Thierry's was a small convenience shop a few blocks over that stocked produce, bread and pastries, several very aromatic cheeses, and of course, wine. The store was called something else, but the locals all referred to it by the name of the garrulous *Marseillais* who ran it.

When Crane stepped into the shop, he was immediately hit in the face with a cloud of very pungent cigarette smoke. Trying not to breathe too deeply, he held the door open for a few seconds to dispel some of the smoke.

"*Hé ! Il fait froid, connard!*" came a shout. "*Merde, c'est moi qui paie l'électricité!*"

"Sorry!" Crane replied, stepping up to the counter with a smile. "It was getting a little thick in here."

Chuckling, Thierry crinkled his pale-blue eyes at Crane as he tapped his ever-present Marlboro against the overflowing ashtray. Behind him, a movie played in English

236

on a portable player balanced atop two high stacks of Hollywood movies. "Hé, *le Canadien*! How is it?" he said, recognizing Crane.

"It's going fine. *Très bien, merci.*" Crane walked over to the wooden table where a few dozen bottles were haphazardly placed. He picked one that was marked €10 and a less nice one priced at €2.50—a sipping wine and a drinking wine. Crane placed both of them on the counter and dug his wallet out of his back pocket.

"And Max? 'E is good?"

Crane smirked, thinking about Max lying on the bloodstained duvet, his ass probably still sore from the strenuous attention it had gotten.

"He's good."

"Ah. Good!" Thierry rang up the wine on his ancient register and held out his hand, accepting Crane's card.

He ran it through the machine, then squinted at the embossed name on the card, his bushy grey brows sliding gradually up his forehead. Lifting his eyes to Crane, he put his hands up imploringly and, with an exaggerated expression of anguish, shouted, "Wilson! Wilson!"

Perplexed, Crane just stared wide-eyed at the man.

Thierry laughed. "You know?" He made the agonized face again. "Noooo! Wilson!"

"I . . . don't know what you're doing."

His expression sobering, Thierry eyed Crane suspiciously. "You know? Like *Castaway*?"

Castaway? "Yeah, I know the movie, but . . ."

"Chuck Noland," Thierry said, pointing to the name on the card. "That's you? You don't hear this a lot?"

Dawning on Crane that Chuck Noland was the main

character's name, he laughed awkwardly. "Ha . . . of course. I was just fooling around." He put on his own expression of despair. "Wilson!" he yelled.

Thierry let out a raspy laugh, doing his impression along with Crane a few more times until Crane felt he'd sufficiently humoured him enough to leave without seeming rude.

"So . . . I'll see you next time." He said, putting the wine bottles carefully into the net shopping bag. "Thanks."

Thierry mimicked putting on a pair of glasses. "You'll be back," he said in a deep voice, obviously making a Terminator joke.

Laughing politely, Crane nodded in parting and left the store. Outside, the air was crisp and cool, and he sucked in deep lungfuls as he walked back to the apartment building where Max and he lived . . . for now, anyway.

It was only when Crane was halfway up the six flights of stairs that something occurred to him. He stopped, one hand on the painted handrailing, and stared ahead.

Castaway.

Crane narrowed his eyes. Max had chosen the name Chuck Noland *long* before Sint Maarten, given that the passport had been waiting for him when they arrived. And he *must* have known the name was from the movie *Castaway*, or . . . was it just a coincidence? Frowning, Crane shook his head. No. There were no coincidences when it came to Max. But, then, did that mean . . .

You're reaching, Doc.

"Am I?" he whispered, his pulse ringing in his ears.

Though Crane hadn't been marooned on a desert island,

he had certainly been left to fend for himself in a strange place with nothing but the clothes on his back. Which meant . . . *Max had been planning on abandoning him all along.* He was a goddamn fucking sentimental imbecile for believing Max's bullshit about this being over a "hesitation."

A low growl escaped from between Crane's lips as he tightened his hold on the railing, his teeth clenched. *I'm going to kill him.*

Crane took the stairs up two at a time and threw open the apartment door. He walked slowly upstairs to the bedroom, his heart beating so hard it felt like it would explode in his chest, and then stopped in the doorway.

Max lay on the bed, the sheets pushed to one side, with his good hand around his erection. The young man was wan, and his eyes were red-rimmed, but his smile was full of warmth.

"I was thinking about you," Max said, his voice husky.

A long drip of precum slid down Max's dick, and Crane watched his nimble fingers spread it down his shaft, then back up to make the head of his cock glisten.

"Come here." Max shuddered out a breath, his eyelids quivering with pleasure as he fondled himself. "I *need* you."

Crane's epiphany about Max's schemes would keep for now—his rage would fuel another violent defilement of Max's body one day soon. But right then, all Crane felt was a deep, overpowering hunger for the young man who had stolen his soul from him.

He wanted only to make the young man tremble and moan in his grasp as he brought him to the brink; he desired only to hear the fervent, prolonged cry that would erupt from deep in Max's chest as he succumbed to his climax.

Would Max whisper his name as his body melted into his touch?

Crane gently deposited the wine on the ground and crawled onto the bed.

"I'm here."

THE END

BOOKS BY BEY DECKARD

FOR AN UP-TO-DATE LIST OF TITLES, VISIT:

https://beydeckard.com/blog/buy-my-books/

MAX, THE SERIES

Max

Max, the Sequel

BAAL'S HEART SERIES

Caged: Love and Treachery on the High Seas

Sacrificed: Heart Beyond the Spires

Fated: Blood and Redemption

Careened: Winter Solstice in Madierus

F.I.S.T.S

Sarge

Murphy

F.I.S.T.S. Handbook For Individual Survival in Hostile Environments

THE ACTOR'S CIRCLE

The Complications of T

The Last Nights of The Frangipani Hotel

THE STONEWATCHERS

Kestrel's Talon

STANDALONE BOOKS

Better the Devil You Know

Exposed

Beauty and His Beast

The Blacksmith's Apprentice

SHORT STORIES

Don't Touch Me (UnCommon Bodies Anthology)

Rakka Surprise (UnCommon Lands Anthology)

ABOUT THE AUTHOR

Artist, Writer, Dog Lover

Bey Deckard is the author of a number of novels including the *Baal's Heart books*, *Max, Beauty and His Beast*, and *Better the Devil You Know*.

Bey lives in Montréal, Canada where he spends most of his time writing, doing graphic work, painting portraits, speaking French, cooking tasty vegetarian eats, or watching more movies than is good for him. If you're the curious type, www.beydeckard.com is where you'll find art and free stories by Bey as well as information on his published works.

bey.deckard@gmail.com
Look for Deckard's Diablerie on Facebook

facebook.com/authorbeydeckard

twitter.com/BeyDeckard

instagram.com/beydeckard

goodreads.com/beydeckard

amazon.com/author/beydeckard

bookbub.com/authors/bey-deckard

Made in the USA
Middletown, DE
22 February 2023

25393714R00144